A GUNFIGHT TOO MANY

Sheriff Sam Hammond, nearing his half-century, sometimes wonders just why he became a lawman. Then the troubles really begin: firstly he narrowly escapes death after a gun battle with rustlers; then the gun-handy range detective Herb Hopkirk shoots dead a rash cowpoke, cripples Sam's deputy, Clint Freeman, and pesters rancher John Snyder's daughter, Sarah. When a mysterious bank robber and a man-hungry widow add to his headaches, is it time for him to quit before he winds up dead?

CHAP O'KEEFE

A GUNFIGHT
TOO MANY

Complete and Unabridged

LINFORD
Leicester

First published in Great Britain in 2008 by
Robert Hale Limited
London

First Linford Edition
published 2009
by arrangement with
Robert Hale Limited
London

British Library CIP Data

O'Keefe, Chap.
  A gunfight too many- -
  (Linford western library)
  1. Western stories.
  2. Large type books.
  I. Title II. Series
  823.9′14–dc22

  ISBN 978–1–84782–699–2

Published by
F. A. Thorpe (Publishing)
Anstey, Leicestershire

Set by Words & Graphics Ltd.
Anstey, Leicestershire
Printed and bound in Great Britain by
T. J. International Ltd., Padstow, Cornwall

This book is printed on acid-free paper

Western
O´Keefe, Chap.
A gunfight too many [large
print]

1

Rustler Trouble

In one sense, Sheriff Sam Hammond was a retiring man. In another, he surely was not.

Sam set no store on bragging, ostentation or swank, unless these peccadilloes could be read into whatever attention he bestowed with the help of the Rainbow City barbershop on the grooming of a fine horseshoe moustache.

But nearing a half-century of largely stormy years — a fair number dedicated to upholding the law in frontier towns of a kind referred to generously as 'wide open' — retiring, as in swopping a working life for one in a rocking-chair, seldom entered his thoughts.

Until a gang of rustlers hit Concho County.

It couldn't have happened at a worse time for the district. Two dry years had burned up the graze. Lush green had given way to scorched yellow. Rainbow Creek, normally a wide and flowing river, had shrunk to a meandering stream through sun-baked mud. In sum, things had become mighty tough.

The unfavourable weather was a strictly local phenomenon and beef prices in big, faraway industrial cities had in the same years slid with an abundance of prime supply from places that hadn't suffered nature's whims. The mercantile in town had stopped giving loan notes to outfits both big and small when the interest payments on them weren't forthcoming. The best properties were heavily mortgaged to the bank.

The threat of foreclosures was very real.

In these pressing circumstances, Sam was prevailed upon by Lorraine Delrose to lie in wait for the increasingly confident and daring rustlers. She swept into his dusty law office in her carefully preserved range-queen finery, doffed a grey Stetson, which she flung down on his paper-strewn desk, and shook loose a fall of jet-black hair untouched by grey.

'Howdy, ma'am,' Sam said, rising to his feet. 'What can we do for you today?'

'Don't be stuffy, Mr Hammond,' she said, with a second toss of her head. ' 'Ma'am' indeed ... to you, it's Lorraine and you know it — Sam.'

But the tilt of her head and the firmness of her chin gave the lie to easy familiarity. Too, Sam had the commonly received impression that the amber eyes looking out from a smooth, impossibly wrinkle-free face the colour of ivory were also looking down.

Maybe it was just a result of her confidence that no woman in the territory could count as yet on looking better than Lorraine Delrose — former singer and the star of a touring troupe which had played opera houses from

San Francisco to Salt Lake City and across the remarkably supportive nineteenth-century West to the river towns of Nashville, Cincinnati, Natchez and New Orleans.

She stripped off a pair of kid riding gloves and slapped them irritably against the palm of her left hand.

'However, I do have business . . . law enforcement business. Evan Gregg tells me fiddlefooted scum are trespassing on the Triple S, lurking in the tree-shadowed nooks and crannies of the hill country. They mean no good, Sam. I want you to raise a posse, round them up. You know I don't have the crew to face down the thieving vermin. No more than anybody else these days.'

Sam continued to regard her calmly, his steady gaze giving nothing away.

'Many men without jobs roundabout and mouths still to be fed. I'm not mounting manhunts for drifters, malcontents or plain hard-luck cases. Not without proof of wrong-doing or less'n I have paper on 'em from other places.

4

Such has the whiff of a wild-goose chase, no matter what your foreman tells you.'

Lorraine was incredulous and affronted.

'So you'll do nothing!' she hissed. Fire flashed in the amber eyes; full breasts heaved.

Sam did admire to see her with her dander up and had been unable to resist the temptation to provoke.

Always lush and statuesque, Lorraine had been, when Sam arrived in Rainbow, the first retired or practising opera singer he'd seen who hadn't been fat and fortyish in looks ahead of years. As he'd become acquainted with his bailiwick and its people, he'd figured how it had come about.

She'd seen what she'd wanted: Rex Snyder and the Snyder cattle-country empire. And she'd renounced unassured celebrity to help herself to it. Today, despite the passing of time, she was more regal than ever. Despite widowhood, she persisted in the use of her original family, or possibly stage, name — just as she had, in fact, during her husband's lifetime. She was 'La Delrose' to the envious who dared to smirk behind her back.

Sam smiled inwardly. Time was long past ripe for the high-handed Lorraine to wake up to certain realities.

He continued as though she hadn't spoken. It would have taken a very keen ear to detect that the ever-present gravel in his voice was a mite less abrasive.

'Howsomever, I'll allow it warrants investigation and to that purpose I volunteer to do some night riding — keeping my eyes peeled and a gun to hand.'

It was Lorraine's turn to permit herself the luxury of a small, secretive smile.

'Well, that's good then, Sam . . . good! Maybe you can have supper with me some time at the Triple S. Leave town duties for once to Deputy Freeman — young Clint, isn't that his given name? You could stay over the night . . . '

She left the suggestion floating among the sun-sparkling motes in the still, close air and turned to leave.

'But first get the job done, huh?'

'Sure. Business before pleasure.'

As long as your rustlers don't send me to meet my Maker, Sam might have added, but didn't. Moreover, he was uncertain about Lorraine's implicit invitation.

For many a long year, romance had played no part in his life. Lawdogging sat uneasily with emotional attachments. An early, brief and tempestuous marriage had taught him that. And, too, attractive offers always had a price . . .

The town's most impenitent madam was Jenny Abernethy. Of mature years and with a gaudy glamour of her own she'd never admit was fading, Jenny had discreetly let it be known to the sheriff that the young ladies of conspicuous charm and flexible morality who boarded at her house regarded him as a handsome gentleman. They would savour the opportunity to oblige him without charge. A peppering of grey in his hair gave him distinction while only incidentally allowing he was old enough to be most of her residents' father.

But because it would be very easy to let himself become entwined in the shapely limbs available, Sam associated with Madame Abernethy and her establishment only at arm's length. He always declined her repeated attempts to donate the girls' tempting generosity.

He pointed out a lawman's pay in Rainbow City didn't stretch to having himself a time, questions might be asked, and some citizens would be unwilling to wink at a sheriff being human. Anyways, it was part of his creed that involvement with women sooner or later led to trouble of one sort or another.

Accordingly, Lorraine's proposition, though not entirely unexpected and appealing at a sensual level to any red-blooded man, was also nothing he could leap at. Or into.

He would have to think long and

hard before he entered a bed in the attractive widow's house.

But Lorraine said, 'I'll be expecting you, Sam.'

⋆ ⋆ ⋆

Sam Hammond told Deputy Clint Freeman he was in for a spell of double shifts as he planned to spend some time out of town, hunting leads on the rustlers.

'Hell of a dismal way for you to do your duty,' Clint said, shaking his head in contemplation of the rigors of the range life he'd turned his back on after a few short years. 'Lonely camp fires and cold dawns. You sure about this?'

'No, I'm not,' Sam said. 'Frankly, I don't cotton to leaving the town in your hands — not because you're incapable, but you're young for the responsibility, and in my experience things have a habit of flaring up in quiet towns just when you don't need them to.'

'You're getting to sound like an old

woman!' Clint joshed good humouredly. 'Even my shoulders are broad enough for this burg. Hell, Sam, it ain't like it was. I remember when I was just a shirt-tail kid it was a real trouble town — a blot on a stretch of lush cattle country with mineral strikes bringing in the riff-raff in droves. Rainbow City: pretty name, ugly place. You fixed all that and made it a peaceable place where honest, hardworking folks could put down roots.'

Sam knew the eulogy was well intended, but he found it embarrassing. He grinned crookedly. 'Weren't quite like that, Clint. The gold and silver petered out.'

'Sure . . . but only *after* you'd been shot at with guns, cut with knives, got yourself stove up in bar-room brawls.'

And Sam couldn't deny there'd been a time when he'd made nearly as many enemies as the county had citizens in the cause of establishing law and order.

But he said, 'My point exactly. There's as good a chance of danger in towns as there is on any range. The lid has to be kept on and you never know when some galoot might take it into his fool or drunken head to lift it. Frontier places are never wholly respectable. Don't take much to disturb the quiet and settled life.'

But Clint's confidence in Sam and his achievements was undented. He was only vaguely aware that a peace officer's pay was scarcely enough to live on and his life could end swiftly and without dignity.

Tall and lanky and still possessed of a certain boyish awkwardness, he said, 'Well, you're the boss, Sam, but it seems to me like you're handing yourself the mucky end of the stick.'

In the event, both men were given a raw deal. Both found themselves facing death.

★ ★ ★

Sam had followed the men from the shadowy hills on to the Triple S range.

11

They were three and the murmur of their voices carried back to him softly on the night air. They had no inkling they'd been followed from their supper camp, that a lawman was planning on catching them red-handed at their rustling game.

Sam figured they were down-and-out cowhands laid off by some outfit hit by the hard times. Once they backed themselves into a corner, he felt he could take them without too much trouble. Wouldn't need any posse to round them up, as Lorraine Delrose had demanded.

Scrub gave way in patches to grazing. The trio closed in on their objective. Fifty head of Triple S yearling beeves. The cattle were bunched in a draw and it would be an easy job for the three to cut themselves out a fair number of the best stock.

The edges and the far end of the draw were heavily choked with brush which Sam used for concealment of a deft approach at a tangent which would converge with the raiders.

Arriving where he wanted to be on the fringes of the brush, he reined in. He checked and filled his right fist with a Colt Peacemaker, waiting. He eased his seat in the leather and saddle trappings creaked in the night.

Although they were making tolerable noise themselves and no attempt to limit it, the small sounds alerted the riders. Before he could rap out the word that he had them covered, the three riders swiftly swung their horses to confront him.

A quarter moon swam from behind thin cloud, augmenting the starlight, casting its light over rock, brush and pasture. And Sam saw shifty eyes and grim mouths set in faces hard and deadly as hatchets. It was then, for the first time, he realized.

These men's open approach was not so much a thing of carelessness as of boldness. He'd miscalculated.

No destitute cowhands these. Poor trash, for sure, but out-and-out killers.

They were strangers to him, but their kind wasn't. They were men who had long ridden on the wrong side of the law. Somewhere, in places down their back trail, they'd probably have made a big reputation for themselves as fast guns. He felt a stab of fear. Why had he taken the fool idea he could cope with this single-handed?

'A sher'ff!' one snapped.

Reaction to the star that winked in the moonlight on his vest was instinctive and immediate. Two of the three clawed for the holstered six-guns at their sides.

It was him or them — Sam fired, blowing one man from his saddle into the dust, without saying a word.

The second outlaw's finger was tightening on the trigger of his gun when Sam shot again, emptying another saddle.

The third man — the slowest — whipped cold, blue steel from leather and was the first and only one of them to loose lead.

Sam was hit somewhere in the upper

left arm or shoulder. He was flung backwards under the impact of the slug, spilled from his saddle with a crash to the hard ground. He sprawled. The bullet wound pumped blood. But the Peacemaker was still gripped in his right hand.

The third man's hesitation, his slowness compared to his companions, was now his downfall. His partners were out of the fight; the sheriff was down, too. Moans filled the air. Who was dead? Who was dying?

It wasn't Sam. He fired back between the legs of his shuffling horse soon as he had a clear target.

On an upward trajectory, the slug passed through the incredulous outlaw's chest and exited at his neck, tearing a gaping hole. The seconds of staring, frozen immobility when he should have been finishing the job on the sheriff with a swift, follow-up blast had cost him dearly.

For a very brief, charged moment, Sam's eyes locked with the shocked man's stare of hate. Then the look became glassy and dead, the sorry life behind it over. He toppled.

Pain surged through Sam from his bleeding arm. Blackness closed in. He fainted.

2

A Dangerous Man

Miss Sarah Snyder of the Diamond S drove alone into Rainbow City in a smart buggy drawn by two high-steppers with polished harness and coats brushed to a silky gleam. The buggy had red-spoked wheels and a black body brought to a high gloss by multiple coats of varnish over black paint. And if her conveyance was a rolling work of art, much the same could be said for Sarah.

Gold curls cascaded in a shining mass from under her fancy bonnet. Her dark-green gown, taut at breasts and hips, was of a fabric and fashionable cut that wouldn't have been out of place in New York.

A sight to behold — a pretty flower before its fullest bloom — she was at the age of growing when a girl became used to the stares of men. Some she appreciated; some she didn't. She got the feeling she had three particular male watchers this sunny morning.

Though self-conscious, Sarah brought her horses to a standstill outside the mercantile with hands as skilful in the handling of the ribbons as in the tying of the one that decorated her bonnet.

Deputy Clint Freeman admired her openly from the shadows of the law office porch, unaware that his total occupation by actions she thought of as unexciting made him appear glassy-eyed and vacant; a little foolish. Clint in most ways met with her approval. He was young, clean and decent. But she regretted that whenever opportunity arose for conversation these days, he came over shuffle-footed, awkward and tongue-tied.

What was it that did that?

Possibly the significance that she also knew his attentive eyes were blue escaped her.

Evan Gregg, foreman of her aunt, Lorraine Delrose's Triple S outfit, was across the main street, outside the hardware store, supervising the loading of purchases on to a buckboard's tray by one of his crew. She didn't miss his furtive, intent glances in her direction.

The face Gregg presented to the world was wooden, but he'd on more than one occasion hinted at personal interest in her. He'd pressed upon her the odd little gift. A token of his esteem, he would say. Somehow, the compliments didn't seem right, the least of it being that he must be fifteen or so years her senior.

There'd been other, disturbing incidents she preferred to forget.

Gregg was an ambitious man whose first loyalty should have been to her aunt, but she suspected he coveted her father, John Snyder's slightly smaller Diamond S. It had a neighbouring chunk of the best land in the district — water better assured, good graze in the main, and woodland timber. Once, in the time of her paternal grandfather, the property — the Triple S and the Diamond S — had been all one. It could be that Gregg's interest had most to do with the fact she would eventually inherit desirable property than with a desire for her person — though she didn't think it too immodest to recognize the strangely frightening presence of that, too.

Further along, on the steps of the hotel, was the third observer. A stranger, his purposeful scrutiny was wholly disconcerting to Sarah.

He was a man of imposing build with straight black hair brushed back from his forehead. His full face was hard; the eyes deep-set. He had a pale yellow complexion that might suggest a long term spent in a penitentiary, but Sarah knew the skin colour to be the kind the West's hottest sun never changed . . . the same way it never made a snake look warm. His bulky body also had no softness in it.

He said something brusquely to an

aproned woman who was cleaning the hotel windows. She glanced in Sarah's direction and replied, whereupon he came striding across the roadway.

The big man's eyes narrowed appraisingly when he approached. He touched the brim of his derby hat perfunctorily. Sarah felt uncomfortable. His mouth was thickly, sensuously lipped, and an old, puckered scar ran from the left cheekbone to its corner.

'Miss Snyder, I understand.' And he grinned like a wolf.

A dangerous man, she summed up. He had an aura that instantly frightened her. It would be playing with fire to allow oneself so much as to show a reciprocal curiosity.

But he'd cunningly corralled her between a hitching rack and her horses. She couldn't move forward without pushing past him — and he would have to be immovable by an average woman. The only escape would be to turn her back completely and walk away in a direction she didn't wish to go. If he'd let her . . .

She was unsure how she should deal with the situation.

In polite society, men didn't force encounters with ladies to whom they'd not been introduced. Likewise, it was generally taught that a good woman didn't introduce herself to a strange man. Should a man appeal to her senses, she still withheld, keeping as secret as she could the glow of her body, the blush on her cheeks. Only the fallen woman — the kind who lived at Jenny Abernethy's girls' boarding-house — resorted to bold, unmistakable signs of invitation, consenting to use the charms of her sex promiscuously, regardless of pleasure or affection, to capitalize on the short supply in frontier communities of female company.

It was, therefore, a small comfort to Sarah that this was happening on the street, in daylight, in public. Surely she was not mistaken for a whore. And why had he found out her name? Alone and in a darker place, she might have panicked, though she wasn't a timid sort.

'I beg your pardon, sir,' she said stiffly. 'You have an advantage over me. Who are you?'

'Name's Hopkirk, Herb Hopkirk, out of Chicago and other places. I'm looking for your father.'

'Well, as you can observe, Mr Hopkirk, I come to town alone.'

'So I see. Where is your pa?'

Rather than relief, Sarah felt a jump of apprehension that quickened her pulses.

'I — I see very little of my father. If you have business, perhaps you should look for him at the Diamond S.'

Hopkirk sneered. 'Spoken like a princess, missy, but it ain't any proper answer to my question.'

Meanwhile, the other eyes on her hadn't missed her dismayed confusion. The two Triple S men and Deputy Freeman converged on the scene.

Evan Gregg got there first. His impassive face was charged with sudden hate.

'This man botherin' yuh, Miss Sarah?' he demanded.

His help had less finesse.

'Back off, mister!' he said bluntly to Hopkirk. 'That's Evan's gal yuh've gotten flustered. He don't stand fer that.'

It was news to Sarah that she was Evan or anyone's girl, but it was no time to disabuse a presumptuous suitor.

Hopkirk turned on Gregg's crewman. His mouth moved grimly. The scar carved from cheekbone to lip was taut and white.

'Ain't any of your business, cowpoke. Nor this gent's. I ain't fixing on catting around with his kitty. Take your sticky beaks someplace else!'

It was then that Gregg laid a meaty left hand on Hopkirk's broad shoulder, turning him and bunching his right fist to take a swing at his derisive face.

Hopkirk's right hand dipped with speed that deceived the eye. It emerged from behind the left breast and lapel of his suit coat closed around the butt of a

Smith & Wesson revolver, which he'd had ready for the swift draw in a concealed shoulder holster.

'I don't mess in fisticuffs,' he growled. 'You want to make an issue of this, I'll give you the chance to fill your own hand with iron.'

That was when Deputy Freeman reached the knot of remonstrating men, and the startled girl he admired, to intervene in the developing quarrel.

'Put the pistol up, sir! Or I'll have to ask you to accompany me to the office and deposit it there. Sheriff Hammond don't hold with gunplay on Rainbow's streets.'

'Well, I'll be . . . ' Hopkirk said, his lip curling. 'Deputy, this — hick was raising fists to me.'

Clint looked to Gregg. 'We don't hold with brawling neither, Mr Gregg,' he said, with even-handed patience modelled on Sam Hammond's technique with troublemakers.

Gregg said sarcastically, 'Sure, sonny boy. Don't know what got into me.'

Hopkirk snarled and put his gun back in its hideout rig under his left armpit where it made a bulge. 'You'll keep, cow nurses.'

The scar on his face was livid but the high colour didn't touch any other part of his hard face.

Sarah said nothing. She was old enough to know a woman's two cents' worth was worth two cents in situations and places like these. She was also woman enough to take a convenient chance when it was offered.

By the time the men had backed off from each other, like separated but bristling dogs denied a fight, she'd raised her fine skirt above her ankles and dashed into the mercantile.

It was for Clint Freeman's best. He'd dealt with the matter efficiently so far, but Sarah didn't want the awkward business of trying to explain to him something she didn't understand herself; that was a little frightening.

Crazy, but once Clint's eyes were on her, and hers on his, it would be sure to wind up in fluster, tied tongues and red cheeks. Apart from anything else . . .

★   ★   ★

The bitterness that had swiftly arisen between the two Triple S men and the man called Hopkirk, a stranger in town, wasn't cured by Clint's intervention and the deputy knew it, though little beyond.

What was the root of the trouble?

What would Sam Hammond do if he was here?

Maybe Sarah could shed some light on the quarrel, but Clint balked at chasing after her on such a chore. It would make him feel crass somehow. He feared he might look like a busybody and therefore awful small in her beautiful eyes.

Sam, Clint decided, would wait and see. No, *watch* . . .

So that was what Clint did.

He was on the law office porch. The Hopkirk *hombre* had retired to the

27

hotel where he was staying. Evan Gregg and the Triple S hand he knew as Chelsum had gone back to loading their buckboard outside the hardware store. And once the job was finished, Clint kept watching as they visited the neighbouring harness shop before repairing to the Gold Pot saloon.

What happened shortly after caused his glimmer of mild concern to flare into alarm. Herb Hopkirk crossed from the hotel to enter the saloon, too.

Had he been watching the cowboys from a hotel window? Was this deliberate? Was he aiming to face them and finish the unsettled exchange they'd had on the street?

Clint never flinched from an awkward situation. He guessed possibilities existed for a ruckus and knew his duty.

His shoulders tautened imperceptibly and he strode across the dusty main drag headed for the Gold Pot. He went wary-eyed and with a right hand swinging close to the assurance of a walnut gun butt. If Hopkirk was fixing on reaching for his underarm hideaway again, surely he couldn't beat a cutback holster draw.

He pushed through the batwing doors into the smoke-laden atmosphere and the hubbub of voices within. The place was only partly full and it took Clint but a moment to pick out where and how trouble was developing at the far end of the long, solid counter.

Leaving the louvred half-doors swinging to and fro behind him, he moved quickly across the room.

'No, we don't aim to drink with no high-handed stranger,' Evan Gregg was saying belligerently. 'Pull your freight, mister! We don't answer no questions. Plain don't need your comp'ny!'

Hopkirk essayed a falsely hearty laugh. 'Well, maybe I started about it the wrong way on the street, Mr Gregg. We don't have to be on diff'rent sides in this. Didn't appreciate a big, grown man like you could have set his sights on the little missy.'

Gregg's jaw clenched; his face got

red. He spluttered. 'What do you mean?'

'But yeah,' Hopkirk went on smoothly, 'I can allow you've gotten it figured right — she'd make a spicy roll in the hay. We could maybe fix that . . . for you and your sidekick both.'

Chelsum had made quick work of a bottle of whiskey. It was already less than half full. Which meant he was more than half full of foolhardiness.

Clint blurted, 'Hold on there!'

But he was too late. Chelsum was insulted and fighting mad. He took his right boot off the bar's sole-polished iron footrail and groped for his gun — little realizing the dire consequences his action would have.

'You sick ol' bastard! Nobody talks to the Triple S that way. I'm gonna get rid of you fer good an' all!'

'Go ahead and try, cowpoke!' Hopkirk rapped, backing off, going into a crouch.

It was all unravelling faster than Clint could keep track, let alone interfere. A sudden, intense silence had replaced the hubbub. Every voice was stilled and every eye was turned toward what was for a split-second a portentous tableau.

Then flame stabbed from a blue-black gun muzzle, the deafening crash of gunfire rocked the saloon and Chelsum pitched forward. Hopkirk was so lightning-fast, his hand had dipped inside his coat front and he'd drawn and fired before Chelsum could squeeze his trigger.

Hopkirk whirled, his back to the fallen man and the counter. His eyes glittered like ice. His scar was a slash of colour on his hard, cold face. His smoking Smith & Wesson menaced the gasping onlookers.

'Everyone saw that — he threatened me, drew on me! Anyone else need a taste?'

'Hold it!' Clint yelled. 'No more shooting. I'm the law here and I'm confiscating that weapon.'

'You again! Back down, law puppy!' Hopkirk snarled.

'Not till I have your hideout.'

'You talking 'bout this?' Hopkirk said, waving the gun.

Clint tried to put firmness into a voice that to his own ears sounded ridiculously youthful.

'I am.'

'That so? Then draw, kid, and see if you really can take it offa me!'

Clint wasn't hunting trouble but he also knew he mustn't show he was scared. He took another step forward.

Though he made no move to pull his own gun from leather, Hopkirk took his advance as sufficient challenge. He didn't give him a chance. His gun was out and he triggered again.

The Smith & Wesson crashed viciously a second time and Clint felt a sudden, excruciating pain in his right leg. He cried out as the impact of the striking slug threw him off his feet. He didn't know whether anyone heard him in the general pandemonium that broke out.

He hit the floor in an untidy heap. He couldn't get up. Everything swam before his eyes. He became aware of men gathering around him; voices and faces full of concern.

'Take him to the sawbones,' someone said.

'We should make a tourniquet pronto,' another said, getting to his knees.

'Yuh shouldn've done that, mister,' the apron said tentatively from behind his counter, ready to duck beneath it.

Hopkirk glared. 'A feller's within his rights. He's got to protect himself in these two-bit cow-towns. The kid deputy was out of line.'

No one had the guts to contradict him. The pain in Clint's leg grew and grew. The light began to go dim. Could you die from a bullet in the leg? Clint knew he was losing blood. His pants leg was wet and sticky, and getting more so.

'I'll be all right in a minute,' he heard his voice say as though from a long way away. Delirium was threatening. If only Sam was here; he'd know what to do. He wanted Sam.

Now where was it Sam had gone? Only Sam could sort out this mess . . .

3

First Aid, Second Thoughts

Some hours earlier, out on the rolling rangeland, Sam Hammond regained his senses. He took deep, calm breaths, reorienting himself.

His opponents, the three rustlers, hadn't fared so fortunately. They wouldn't be checking their wounds. They were dead.

Sam cut the bloody left sleeve of his shirt from his arm. The arm was sore but no great damage had been done. The bullet had sliced through skin and a little flesh but the blood was already congealing in the furrow, albeit he couldn't have lost consciousness for long.

The earliest of first light was tingeing the lower rim of the eastern sky a lemony grey. Being closer to the Triple

S headquarters than to town, Sam decided to head first for Lorraine Delrose's ranch house where he could receive first-aid for his injury and report that a raid on her cattle had been thwarted. Maybe Lorraine's complaint had been dealt with for good and all.

But he had no grounds for smugness or self-congratulation, and this he was to tell the woman who came out herself in answer to his hullo of the house.

The Snyder family had once been people of substance, eating high on the hog, though in Lorraine Delrose's widowhood the days of opulence had passed and the outfit now functioned on a shoestring. A skeleton crew rode line, after a fashion, and additional men were hired in lean numbers for roundups. The ranch-house stood on an elevation surrounded by a sprawl of corrals, barn, bunkhouse and a half-dozen smaller buildings. None of the lesser, workaday structures were positioned so as to detract from the dominance of the main house, built in the wealthiest of times with fluted columns, covered gallery and formal, wide steps.

Lorraine had pulled on a shawl over her night-gown.

'Sam!' she exclaimed. 'And you're hurt.'

'It's nothing bad,' Sam said. 'Where's Evan Gregg? I'll ask him to bandage it up properly.'

'He left for town with Chelsum just minutes ago. Some supplies need bringing out. But come in, do. I'll fix your arm myself.'

'I'm not hurt bad,' he repeated. 'Except maybe in peace of mind.'

He followed her down the main passage and into a small, personal room that she used for dressing and her toilet. It was furnished with a big mirror, a wash-stand, and shelves of bottles, brushes, trinkets and feminine knick-knacks. A small rolltop desk, open, held personal stationery, pen and ink bottle and a roll of red tape.

She sat him on the round-cushioned

chair. Through another half-open door, he found himself facing her bedroom. The covers on the bed had been thrown aside hurriedly, carelessly. He thought he could see the deserted impression of her body on the undersheet and mattress. It suggested warmth and invitation.

'Tell me what happened,' she said.

He told her the bare facts of the exchange of gunfire on the Triple S range and its outcome. But Lorraine had a way of coaxing a man to spill his troubles, of saying maybe more than he wisely should. She'd let her shawl slip from her shoulders to the floor as she applied a stinging antiseptic lotion to cleanse his wound. The thin stuff of her nightgown clung disturbingly to the full curves of her lush body.

'Hell, I bungled the job,' Sam finished gruffly. 'I ought to be kicked out of office, and it'd be no bad thing. Only reason I'm alive is I was hit in this shoulder first and dumped out of the saddle. Sure, one day, the tin badge, making the same fool of myself, and slowing reactions are going to get me killed. I'll've gotten myself into a gunfight too many. Maybe I should be thinking about resigning.'

Lorraine bent over him and the loose neckline of her gown sagged. He couldn't help but see large, unrestrained globes of flesh tipped startlingly with dark nipples, swollen and stiff, before he averted his gaze. He tingled and his pulses raced.

'You're too hard on yourself, Sam. You stopped the rustling and probably saved the county a lot of trouble.'

'They should've had their day in court,' Sam persisted jerkily.

Lorraine said, 'I care nothing about that. Stands to reason dead rustlers are the best sort to have. You'll think more clearly after you've rested. There's no rush to get back to town and I've got to thank you. Show I'm grateful . . .'

'The first-aid is as much as I deserve.'

' . . . that you are appreciated, Sam,' she plunged on, 'whatever you might think about yourself. You know what I mean. Why not come and lie on my bed for a spell?'

The tingle became a heat. Sam got a little red in the face. 'I don't think I should do that, Lorraine.'

'Oh, don't be so puritan, Sam. We're not kids. We're both adults well along in years.'

'Yeah,' Sam grunted, 'You're right 'bout that.'

Sam was no moralizer, but he was aware Lorraine didn't subscribe to the standards upheld — in public at least — by the polite society of their time. She'd attempted before a limited discussion of a woman's sexual needs at her admitted age of forty-one, professing she knew this time of life presented a woman with the peak of passion's demands; confessing that her passion was at war with her rationality and dignity; declaring she would feel no shame in giving its expression a looser rein.

She said, 'There's nothing like a proper caring-for to make a real man feel good about himself, forget his troubles. What the world doesn't see doesn't hurt it.'

Sam took a deep breath. 'Then again, the world *does* get to know these things, and proper caring-for ain't what some folks would call it. It could harm your reputation.'

'A fig for reputation!'

But Sam disregarded her snort of derision. Doggedly, he rose to his feet and picked up his hat.

'Well, thank you kindly for the nursing and I'll be on my way . . . taking the ride gentle, of course.'

He was serious about what he'd said before the conversation had veered out of hand. He'd survived the shootout with the rustlers by a wild, odds-against chance. It was high time to reconsider his options. They didn't, couldn't include even a fleeting spell of intimacy with Lorraine Delrose, tempted though he was by her unmistakable overtures.

Should he hand in his badge?

Somehow, he didn't see a retired

sheriff down on his uppers being much of a long-term interest for a woman like Lorraine Delrose. He figured the willing lady, alluring as she might be, was already struggling to come to terms with reduced circumstances.

She went out with him to his horse, clinging, her solicitude becoming a hurt and disappointment of her own.

'Let loose my good arm, Lorraine. I'm steady enough on my legs — it weren't one of them got creased.'

He mounted up, a mite awkwardly, they exchanged 'so longs' with smiles that were forced for different reasons and he started out.

'You come see me again by and by!' she called after him.

'When I can . . . ' he said noncommittally.

On the lonely ride, he set to thinking about her and her big, soft bed. Damn it, she was no spring chicken but she was still all woman and eager to prove it.

He cussed himself alternately for his

inhibitions and — because he'd been reminded by the gunfight that he was getting along in years, maybe nearing the end of his working life as a lawman — for being a useless, randy old man.

Now invitation and temptation were behind, he regretted he hadn't satisfied his curiosity and undimmed instincts. In her bed, he might have gotten her out of his head. Him out of hers, too.

But behind it all, was the thought that he'd come close to meeting his death. One more gunfight like he'd just had could be the death of him. Again, he wondered at the arithmetic of the odds. Perhaps the question he should be confronting was not whether he wanted to retire but whether he wanted to go on living.

Fate had given him a second chance this time. Next time it might not.

★ ★ ★

The sun was high and Sam was tired, thirsty and hungry when he rode into

Rainbow City. Town had looked good from the distance, a welcoming speck that had grown steadily larger, but when the trail became the main street, the tired collection of mostly frame buildings, many small and in need of paint, didn't look so grand in his eyes. An unnatural quietness hung about the place. And what was this?

The door and windows of his office were tightly closed.

He was puzzled. He frowned, turning over in his uneasy mind the quickly forming notion all was not well.

He called out to a street urchin walking a pulling puppy with plaited string for a lead.

'Has Deputy Freeman been called out of town, button?'

'Nope. He's bin carried on an ol' door to the doc's, Sher'ff,' the boy said, wide-eyed with the excitement of the news he had to convey. 'Yuh missed all the hullabaloo. There was gunplay in the Gold Pot an' a man was kilt!'

It was more than the dust and heat

that made Sam's throat and mouth feel rough as sandpaper.

'Clint Freeman's hurt?' he croaked. The thought that his young assistant had run into major trouble during his absence hit him like a club. His own grazed arm was immediately forgotten.

'Shot in the leg. Mebbe he'll be a *gimp*,' the urchin imparted in pitiless wonder.

Sam left his horse still saddled at the hitch rail outside the office and hurried to the small clinic run by the Rainbow City medico back of the barbershop. He would see to stabling and feeding the horse later.

'What's happened to Clint Freeman?' he demanded.

The barber's wife, who worked as the doctor's nurse, said the deputy was uncomfortable but conscious and had best tell the story himself.

Wincing from pain, and mighty miserable over his perceived failure to keep the peace in town, Clint gave his account from a plank bed in a room

44

that reeked of carbolic.

'I was in a fix,' he concluded. 'Chelsum called this Hopkirk gent a bastard and went for his gun. Hopkirk had reasonable excuse to defend hisself. I demanded his gun and he took it as a challenge. I don't know the law on such fine points, but folks are saying the stranger acted within his rights.'

Grudgingly, Sam recognized a certain code had been followed. To secure a proper hold of the facts of a saloon fracas after the event was never easy. Minds blurred by liquor at the time and carried away by embellishments later made for poor witnesses in any court, let alone a court on the frontier. By the time of the next sessions, his honour the judge might be disposed to dismiss the case as too weak to have been brought.

Sam well knew the powers and limitations of his office, but he said, 'I'll be going to have a word with this Hopkirk. We don't need a troublemaker in town. What's he here for anyhow?

And why, first off, was he accosting Miss Snyder?'

'Can't figure it, Sam. Damn it, I never got the excuse to ask what was really going on before I was knocked right offa my feet.' Clint grimaced as he shifted his splinted and bandaged leg. 'Doc says the bone's damaged. I'll be laid up mebbe six weeks.'

Sam groaned inwardly. He'd be short-handed a long time. And would six weeks be the end of it? Or would Clint be permanently crippled, as the boy on the street had suggested?

He hoped not.

★   ★   ★

Sam didn't waste any time. His horse stabled, he went to Chai-Lee's restaurant where he ordered a very late breakfast of ham and eggs and a stack of pancakes. He drank one cup of coffee while he waited for the meal; another after. The inner man served, he hied him to the hotel where he was told he'd find Mr Herbert Hopkirk in Room 3.

Upstairs front, Sam reflected — one of the best in the establishment. His knock was answered with a rapped 'Come in.'

The occupant was seated by the window, smoking a cigarette, with a chunky square bottle and a whiskey glass to hand on the floor beside him. The picture of a city man at his leisure. He was in shirtsleeves with a yellow cravat tucked into a plush, buff waistcoat, both of which served to highlight an unhealthy complexion.

Sam noted the scar, right down to observing the small pocks either side that might have been the places where stitches once had been inserted.

'Mr Hopkirk?'

Relaxed in manner, Hopkirk's eyes alighted on Sam's badge with a momentary glint. He nodded and gestured his guest to a facing chair and spoke lazily.

'Howdy, Sheriff. Set yourself down.

Or this could shape up as one hectic day. Sure is a town on a short fuse you have here.'

He offered his visitor no drink, no cigarette. He didn't ask the purpose of Sam's visit, though that might have been because it was obvious. He didn't ask what he could do to help.

Sam hadn't liked the sound of him from before the start. His smug attitude wasn't changing his mind.

'Nothing much wrong with my town,' he said combatively.

Hopkirk dragged on his cigarette and blew smoke rudely in Sam's face.

'You don't know the half of it, Lawman.'

Sam didn't flinch. Narrowing his eyes, he digested the comment and ignored the smoke.

'You know more'n I know about Rainbow City I'd be surprised, mister. Talk straight, starting with what your real business is here — if it ain't picking gunfights with folks going legally about theirs.'

Hopkirk grinned like a wolf might grin. A showing of teeth in a sneer.

'I'm a private detective.'

'With the Pinkerton Agency?'

'Nope . . . was, but not now. You could call me a freelance range dick and enforcer.'

'So . . . ' Sam said, nodding his understanding, 'a bully-boy hired by ruthless cattlemen's clubs bothered by settlers and meaner mining companies with labour troubles.'

'Not this time, Sheriff. I'm here to do the job regular law officers like yourself are incapable of.'

'That right? What would it be?'

'I'm here to trap a notorious bank robber and claim a share of a fat reward.'

4

Girl in Troubled Waters

Sam Hammond shook his head in disbelief. The only part he could comprehend was that the scar-faced detective was admitting to being, in fact, a bounty hunter. It was a trade that attracted the lowest, deadliest scum.

In 1873 the Supreme Court had defined the rights of bounty hunters as agents of bail bondsmen, authorized to deliver up miscreants who'd skipped. They could pursue the subject into another state or territory and enforce the original imprisonment. They could arrest the wanted man on the Sabbath. If necessary, they had the right to break and enter a house.

In reality, the bounty hunter in the West was a ruthless mercenary, meting out frontier retribution with a blazing gun and a cold will, dispatching criminals for the reward money on their heads without thought of bringing them to formal, conventional justice.

Sam said drily, 'A bank robber? In this small town? You've got to be mistaken, Hopkirk. Rainbow don't keep more'n small change in its bank these days. It holds more of its customers' notes than gold eagles and greenback bills. There ain't sufficient in it to tempt serious hold-up artists. Would scarce pay 'em to bother. Times are hard.'

'Did I say the man was here to rob your bank?' Hopkirk said with harsh scorn.

'Not exactly,' Sam answered. 'Nor named him.'

Hopkirk turned sly.

'Maybe I can't. Some smart-aleck newspaper writer has dubbed him 'Dick Slick' on account of his quick and smooth hold-ups. Slick is apt — he goes in and out of banks and quits their towns like a greased hog.' He smirked.

''Course, the newshound might've had some other analogy on his mind.'

'Aah . . . I've been sent dodgers on the very feller,' Sam said. But he remembered he hadn't tacked up the wanted posters since without a clear picture or the tolerable detail necessary for identification they hadn't seemed worthy of display. 'Nothing in the paper on him suggested Rainbow figures on Slick's range, though I allow his gang ain't let off light a wide scatter of towns from Sacramento, California, to Lewiston, North Idaho.'

Hopkirk's disdain lessened none. 'Maybe Dick Slick doesn't hanker to plunder this town for some good reason, Sheriff — like he uses your bailiwick for a hideout between jobs.'

The notion a notorious bank robber might be in Rainbow was startling. Slick had been sought a number of years but he'd always managed to give the law the slip. He appeared three or four times a year, committed his armed robberies, paid off his recruits with stolen dollars and disappeared again. The conclusion was he changed his identity, making his criminal forays when he had to have more cash to support another, ostensibly innocent life. But people had died brutally and a $3,000 reward had been proclaimed for Dick Slick, alive or dead.

'You're after him for the reward money — a bounty hunter in plain words,' Sam accused.

'I'll say no more than I've been hired in connection with the hunt by a certain party in possession of information.'

Sam studied on the evident refusal to be forthcoming. His estimation was that Hopkirk was no more straight than a wriggling snake. He tried another approach.

'I hear you asked after a lady here and gave offence to her on the street. A Miss Sarah Snyder, a young woman of good reputation.'

Sardonic amusement twisted Hopkirk's lips. 'More than one side to any story, Sheriff.'

'So what's yours?'

'I wanted to talk to her.'

'About your business with Dick Slick?'

Hopkirk shrugged. 'Maybe that's private — for me to know and you to find out, if you can or should. Maybe it's just that I admire the fresh, sparkling and lively attractiveness found in young women outside of large cities.'

Sam didn't cotton to being baited, especially by the man who might have crippled his inexperienced deputy with a lack of justification he'd be hard put to prove.

He sucked in a sharp breath but kept his tongue still.

Hopkirk stubbed out the acrid butt of his cigarette. 'Now, will that be all for now, Sheriff?'

'Sure. For now,' Sam said harshly. 'I've no stomach for bandying words with anyone. But let me tell you this: you've caused more trouble in my town in a day than I should rightly accept for a year.'

Hopkirk widened his heavy-lidded eyes.

'No . . . ? Well, that's bad, ain't it?' He contrived to sound chastened. 'Guess I just don't know how a man should behave among your impetuous, wild-west citizenry. I do beg pardon.'

But Sam wasn't deceived by his mock apology. Privately — ice-cold with anger — he resolved to keep as close a watch as he could on Hopkirk till he showed his real hand or left town.

★ ★ ★

It was six o'clock the next morning before Sam was able to note anything that might be significant in Hopkirk's conduct around Rainbow City.

Less than a half-hour after dawn, Sam was in Chai-Lee's restaurant, today at a more fitting hour for breakfast. First light was creeping through the cracks in and between the falsefronts of the clapboard buildings

55

opposite when Hopkirk made an appearance on the shadowed street.

He went to the livery barn and shortly reappeared mounted on a rented gelding.

Where was the self-styled detective riding, and why?

Sam meant to find out. He swallowed what was left of his coffee, slapped coins on the counter, called his thanks to Chai-Lee and went swiftly to saddle up his own horse.

Hopkirk's tracks were easy to follow. He took the main trail out of town in the direction of Rainbow Creek. Soon, he was in sight and Sam reined in his horse some. He let the lone rider disappear four or five times after that, but always there was the faint banner of his risen dust.

Sam didn't figure on catching up with the man. His agile brain, refreshed by sleep, was deep in conjecture. He couldn't understand what Hopkirk was at, but the road they were on did take them toward the home lot of the

Diamond S, where Sarah Snyder lived.

The chances were strong Hopkirk had it in mind to pick up again the pestering he'd been obliged to drop yesterday.

Hopkirk let up when he reached the ranch buildings, circling them as he reconnoitred. Dogs restrained by clinking chains set up a clamour of barking and a plump housewoman waddled out on to a porch, huffing.

Sam drew into the cover of a clump of closely spaced cottonwood trees. He was too distant to hear distinctly the words of Hopkirk's exchange with the woman, but he had the impression she was agitated by his demanding tone.

Finally, as his manner grew more threatening, the woman pointed to the green and shaded area through which the creek threaded its way.

Hopkirk pulled the gelding's head around and dug in spurs. The servant called after him.

'Must be powerful impo'tant. 'T'ain't

right, suh, I do vow an' declare! I done tol' yo' — Miz Sarah am owed her *privacy*.'

And, as he drew further away, the browbeaten woman yelled after him defiantly something Sam recognized as being from Scripture.

' . . . *for everyone that exalteth hisself shall be abased; and he that humbleth hisself shall be exalted!*'

The clamorous dogs renewed their barking.

Sam grinned to himself. The lady knew her Good Book. She couldn't be faulted aside from a minor slip of pronunciation, excusable with her temper righteously aroused. She stamped back into the house.

He continued to shadow Hopkirk at a distance. He figured his guess was right and Hopkirk intended to speak again with Sarah Snyder. Maybe the girl was gone walking or picnicking, though it seemed early in the day for the latter.

The woodland became thicker and

presently, closer to the water course, impassable on horseback.

Hopkirk cast about, then dismounted and tethered the rented gelding. Steps had been hacked in a narrow, steep tributary gully that descended to the creek. Hopkirk continued down on foot, and was soon hidden from sight. Negotiating the overgrown path wasn't easy. It entailed pushing aside brambles, drooping branches of hackberry, other whippy stuff. Sam heard cussing.

Sam left his horse on a convenient patch of bunch grass. Below, he glimpsed a creek of clear water running over a wide gravel bottom. Upstream, he knew, a fault in the earth hereabout — a slip possibly in time past, now healed and concealed by lush growth — had formed a pleasant, deep hollow, an ideal place to bathe and swim. On three sides, perpendicular walls rose twenty to thirty feet above the surface of a sparkling pool.

Sam realized this was where Hopkirk was headed.

* ★ ★

The swimming hollow was a spot where Sarah Snyder could be at peace with the world. She floated on her back, making lazy backstrokes. The water was cool and clean, its surface alternately dappled with leafy tree shadows and reflected sunlight. It swirled and chuckled, friendly and peaceable but sort of alive.

She loved, too, the colourful wild-flowers that grew in clusters on the shelving banks. From mid-June to early September, Indian paintbrush abounded, its tubular, narrow flowers in bunches. Red was the commonest colour but white and yellow, pink and orange, lent variety. Adding to the visual symphony were magnificent scarlet gilia — trumpet-shaped and vivid — big clusters of bluish-purple lupins, and radiant, sunflower-yellow arnica blooms fully four inches across.

The place was delightful, a bower put together by nature exclusively for someone like herself with the time and sensibility to appreciate it.

For a short while she could forget the bundle of newspaper cuttings. They'd been pressed upon her by her aunt's foreman with his urging she should read them and think about them carefully.

Sarah didn't like to think about Evan Gregg — even his name. She preferred to regard him as the Triple S range boss. This was tantamount to denial, she knew. Evan Gregg had very different ideas about her. He had a personal interest coupled, she shrewdly suspected, with her status as the sole future heiress to the Diamond S.

Her father's holdings were slightly smaller in acreage than her aunt's but they included a good chunk of the very best land in the district, offering better than the Triple S ever would — a guaranteed water supply, good graze and woodland timber.

If she shivered inwardly it had nothing to do with the pleasant coolness of the natural pool; everything to do with Evan Gregg's ambitions. And the way he had of looking at her . . . assessing, coveting all that wasn't his, which was plainly more than a cattle outfit. It didn't help a girl's serenity any to think closely on such things. Some of what he'd said to her in the past, she preferred to leave forgotten.

She put away with special determination memory of an incident following a certain town dance. Evan Gregg was *old* — well, a good fifteen years her senior anyhow. The idea of him having a romantic interest in her was repulsive.

Hearing herself called 'Evan's gal' in town the previous day had confirmed her worst fears about the foreman's persistence, however it might have been overshadowed by the scary approach of the big man with the scarred face who'd said he was looking for her daddy.

Herb Hopkirk had struck her as the kind of stranger parents would want to keep away from their small children.

She'd led a sheltered, privileged life, and knew it, but at 17 and a western-born girl she wasn't without a deal of practical knowledge of the hardness of the world and its sinfulness. The respect accorded her sex in frontier communities was a thin, hypocritical veneer inspired largely by the dispro-portion of nubile women to fiercely competitive men. Look what happened to the girls without male protectors, particularly girls of non-Anglo-Saxon race. They were assumed to be socially inferior and fair game for men's lusts. Prostitution thrived openly, even in Rainbow City.

On a primal level, she felt that something bad was about to happen to her, too; even that it should.

Today, she'd been so disturbed just by Evan Gregg's manner and words that she'd been unable as yet to study the newspaper cuttings, which were an implied accusation; a shot aimed at her life's undeserved security.

The matter of the dates, to which

he'd asked her to pay attention, didn't amount to anything, of course, but she didn't have to wonder what his purpose was.

He'd made that abundantly clear. He'd urged her to submit with good grace to the thing he desired as it would be better for her. He'd been so stolid and insistent, she'd finally, guiltily accepted the small, red-taped bundle of browning paper as a means to finish his visit, to send him on his way, deferring consideration.

She'd cringed when he'd taken her hand in his own sweaty paw and squeezed it as though in some secret confidence. Ugh!

Suddenly, a series of urgent, flute-like gurgling notes pierced the air, going down the scale.

Kingfishers, hummingbirds and common golden-eye ducks lived all along the creek, but this was the call of the meadowlark. Sarah knew several pairs were nesting at the fringe of the woods, each with their own territory from which they noisily chased away intruders. They nested on the open grassland in a depression which the female lined with soft, hairy material and roofed over with a waterproof dome of grass and plant stems.

She considered the birds distinctively pretty. About nine inches long, they had long, pointed bills, brown and black wings and backs, and bright yellow bellies and throats with a black V-shaped bib. She wouldn't want to scare them away.

She'd carefully avoided disturbing the nesting area on her way to the pool, but now not one but at least two males were raising protests.

Was someone coming?

Then — oh, no! — through the trees and undergrowth she heard her answer in the sound of men's voices. Loud, as though raised in argument.

Sarah's heart beat furiously. She rolled over in the water in a splashing flurry and struck out for the bank. To be surprised here would involve at the very least a loss of dignity, and dignity was very dear to her.

Beyond that, she dreaded to think what men might do to a girl in her state in an isolated spot.

Her beautiful, mail-order catalogue clothes all lay carefully folded together with a towel on the bank.

Sarah was bathing naked.

5

The Bare Truth

Sam followed the sounds of Herb Hopkirk's cussing progress through the thick green growth till both abruptly ceased.

He wondered what could have been capable of putting a stop to the big man's haste and bad humour, and continued in his tracks with greater caution.

He drew near enough to see the cause. Hopkirk had fetched up below Sam on a ledge below that overlooked the swimming hole. Sarah Snyder was floating on her back in the shimmering water. She was reason enough to give any man pause.

Stripped of every scrap of her fancy clothes and wearing no bathing costume, she was as pretty as ever. Prettier.

Without adornment, the girl lost her sophistication. She seemed younger than her years, naïve and simple.

Hopkirk seemed fully content for the moment to play the Peeping Tom, as well he might. Sam thought he heard a low, growling chuckle of appreciation and was about to betray their presence to the unsuspecting young miss with a warning shout when somebody else yelled, 'Hopkirk, you bastard! Get your dirty eyes offa that gal afore I thrash you!'

It was the voice of Evan Gregg.

Sam sensed the makings of a fine how-de-do. What was Evan Gregg's explanation for being here? If it was that he'd come to spy on Sarah Snyder, his indignant protest had to be a remarkable case of the pot calling the kettle black.

Hopkirk swung round, his pallid face darkening a shade in anger at being surprised.

'Well, damn me, if it ain't the range-boss Romeo!' he sneered. 'Or should that be Lothario? She's built nice in the right places, ain't she? Long time since I seen a more tempting carcass laid out for free looking.'

Provoked, Gregg smashed through the last, thin screen of bushes that divided them. He was roaring in fury.

'You stinking, low-down pervert!'

He flung himself at Hopkirk, fists windmilling.

Hopkirk grabbed for his concealed Smith & Wesson, but the moment it was whipped from the holster Gregg's unhesitating attack sent it flying from bruised fingers before it was cocked.

Sam figured it was a tolerably even match with no party more sinned against than sinning. They were both too old for innocent romance with Sarah Snyder. Neither of them looked upon her with the kind of worshipful admiration he sometimes saw on the open face of young Clint Freeman, who would have surely died of vivid, blushing embarrassment to see her in a state of nature.

Nobody had business to be prying into the girl's seclusion. That was sheer monkey business. Maybe he should let the pair slug it out.

They closed and several solid thumps sounded meatily. Hopkirk's fist grazed the foreman's ear. Gregg replied with a blow to Hopkirk's chin which lifted it with a sharp, tooth-crunching noise.

But Hopkirk merely shook his head as though to clear it. Undazed, he threw a hard blow to Gregg's neck, and followed it up with another to the solarplexus before the range-man got in close again.

As they came grappling into plainer view on the ledge, dealing each other's ribs a merciless pummelling, Sarah reached the bank below. She flung her left arm ineffectively across her high, bobbing breasts, put her right hand over her neat, virginal cleft and thus made an awkward dash to the pile of her discarded garments.

Here she paused and bent over,

inadvertently displaying the firm globes of a pert rear. In the immodest instant, she snatched up only the towel before racing on.

Her slender, long legs flashed rapidly beneath the towel's scarcely adequate protection, and she ran, hot and furious, into the cover of the bushes without having uttered a single cry.

The two fighters enjoyed none of this sight of sights. Only Sam did, who had eyes for detail sharper than men half his years. No one cheered; no one hooted with lewd laughter. In fact, Hopkirk and Gregg crashed to the ground, panting harshly, fists still swinging, each intent only on overpowering the other. They struggled in the dust, rolling, clawing, each striving to gain the upper hand.

Gregg got astride Hopkirk and grabbed him two-fisted by the hair, his intention to bash his foe's head against the rock. His bruised and bloody face was contorted in a mask of rage.

Hopkirk's clutching hand groped

blindly for his revolver which lay close by.

With the girl gone, Sam decided it was high time for him to do his duty as sheriff of the county, maybe prevent a murder and restore some peace.

He drew a Colt and fired over their heads.

'Let it ride, the both of you!' he bellowed into the dying echoes. 'Miss Snyder's left.'

Startled, the battered combatants separated and got unsteadily to their feet. They looked a real mess. Their clothes were dusty; Gregg's shirt was torn; Hopkirk's derby was flattened.

Six-gun still out and pointed, Sam strode down to join them. He scooped up the Smith & Wesson, broke it open, spilled its loads, which he pocketed, and then handed the harmless weapon it back to Hopkirk.

'I don't rightly know what this is about, gents, but I suggest you leave likewise, in separate directions. And quit pestering Miss Snyder. I aim to go see if she wants to lay a complaint.'

Hopkirk snorted. 'She ain't got the grounds, Mister Sheriff! Not by any letter of the law.'

'Who says yuh wasn't fixin' to ravish her?' Gregg said. 'Sure looked like a man with raisin' petticoat on his mind to me!'

Hopkirk contrived to smirk sarcastically despite split and swollen lips.

'She wasn't wearing a petticoat. Nor a stitch of anything else. Maybe your demure Miss Snyder, who acts in town like butter wouldn't melt in her mouth, ain't so green to the ways of the world; she was showing out all her sweet parts. Remember? Maybe the facts are she's been initiated prior into the paphian pleasures of their usage and it was me that spoiled your sport.'

Evan Gregg reddened, made madder than hell.

'By God, don't try out-coyotin' me with your fancy words, yuh sonofa-bitch — '

'Enough!' Sam roared. 'Get outa here

73

afore I lose my temper, too! Or I might just arrest someone for disturbance of the peace.'

Gregg shrugged and scowled before moving off in shuffling boots.

'He ain't got me buffaloed,' he muttered darkly and so low Sam couldn't be certain of the threat. 'I'll get around to him, you'll see.'

Hopkirk ignored him. He said to Sam, 'Perhaps you might also arrest the young lady for committing a public nuisance, though I've got private business with the high-and-mighty miss and I'll take care of it yet.'

'Then you'll do it in the right place and with Miss Snyder agreeable,' Sam said gruffly. 'I suggest you ride back to town.'

Hopkirk snarled through set teeth, 'It'll have to wait, I guess.'

The detective stomped back along the overgrown track the way he'd come.

Sam recognized either man could be a sore loser and might resume their quarrel some other place. Was he getting soft in letting this go?

He wondered if he didn't ought to chase the provocative, gun-happy Herb Hopkirk out of the county before there was another death, but he had a feeling the man wouldn't chase easily.

He decided he had no responsibility to protect either Evan Gregg or Hopkirk, but Sarah Snyder might be a different case. He went over to her neat pile of clothes and gathered it up. He could pay a visit to the Diamond S on the pretext of returning the stuff.

It was good quality clothing from city stores — frock, chemise, drawers and stockings trimmed with delicate lace, pretty calfskin boots . . . The intimate garments gave off a faint, fresh, floral perfume. A needful man could drive himself crazy handling the silky things and allowing his imagination to run riot. She'd divested herself of everything but, as he'd witnessed, without chaste concealment and adornment of her feminine assets she'd been as perfect as anyone could picture.

He would go easy on the girl. She was what? Likely not more than seventeen summers. A child really, and he'd no doubt as innocent sexually as Hopkirk had tried to suggest to Gregg she wasn't.

What was a mystery to him was the roll of newspaper cuttings, tied with red tape, that he found had been left under the similarly abandoned clothes. He'd seen tape exactly like the piece used someplace before, very recently, but couldn't remember where.

He undid the slipknot. Each cutting contained a report, some with dates ringed in pencil, about the doings of a bank robber.

Dick Slick.

★   ★   ★

The clucking housewoman's face was set in grim, scandalized lines.

'I never known sich goin's-on. High-handed men a-comin'. Miss Snyder stormin' back inta th' house wearin' on'y a towel t' keep from sinfulness.'

Sam nodded sympathetically. 'Needs clearing up.'

'Young mistress am mighty grumpy. Yo' sure she wan' t'see any man, Mistah Hammon'? C'd be she throw a real fit!'

'Please call her, ma'am, and I'll take the risk. The house is big enough, you can go about your chores someplace else while I visit with her. Just trust me.'

'I done always trus' yo', Sher'ff. I jus' don' wan' hear no mo' fussin' an' flouncin' . . . '

Sarah came to the big parlour of the Diamond S ranch house, crossing the polished floor with a quick patter of dainty feet.

She was attired in a quickly assumed checked shirt and Levis, but her hair showed signs of disarray, and quick fingers had missed one of the shirt's most strategic buttons, leaving a distracting gap of which she was — happily — unaware.

'Please sit, Mr Hammond. I can't think why you should have come, but it won't be the first thing I don't rightly understand today . . . not by a long chalk!'

Sam indicated the clothing he'd placed on a mahogany table, part of the dignified colonial decor.

'I brought back your possessions,' he said.

She reddened and a hand went to her mouth.

'Oh! I'm sorry, Mr Hammond. I must have left them at the pool.' Her train of reconstructive thought was visible. She gulped. 'I — I was in a hurry,' she ventured probingly.

'You certainly were, young lady.'

She coloured some more, realizing he might know more than he'd volunteered.

'It was Evan Gregg and that stranger, Hopkirk. They surprised me. Did you see — much?'

'Some,' Sam conceded lightly, 'but I had my hands full separating them sneaky galoots and sending 'em on their way.'

'Why, I didn't realize . . . ' she said, all endearing confusion. 'I'm grateful to you. It's possible you could have saved an unsuspecting girl's honour. That was the second time Hopkirk has come up on me, and Evan Gregg is positively a continuing nuisance. He believes I could fall in love with him, but it's quite out of the question. I'm hardly more than a child.'

Sam thought she told no lie there, though she had as much as any full woman had ever needed to captivate a man. He'd seen the bare truth of it, and for a fact many Western girls her age were wedded, bearing much older husbands' children and being turned early into drudges by house- and ranch-keeping.

Sam figured it best to let lie the subject of her youth, her thoughtlessly revealed beauty and her appeal to men many years her senior.

It was time to produce the newspaper cuttings.

He pulled the roll from a pocket in

back of his pants. He thought she started a little, as though she had until now forgotten she'd left the papers with her clothes, but she recovered quickly and stood there with her head tilted to one side in an attitude of enquiry.

'What do you have there?' Her blue eyes reflected something more than innocence.

'I think you must have seen them before,' Sam said quietly. 'They were with your clothes. Why? What's your interest in Dick Slick, a bank robber and killer?'

From being merely guarded, she went to agitated annoyance. She stepped back from him, as though rejecting the papers he was holding out to her.

'Why have you come here?' Her voice climbed an octave. 'What do you want really? Take the silly cuttings away! They're not mine. I don't want to see them again!'

Sam was astonished at the loss of her normal equilibrium. He could see she was trembling on the edge of fear. He went forward and fastened his firm hands on her arms.

'Please don't get upset with me, Miss Snyder. Get a grip on yourself and tell me what they mean to you.'

'Nothing!' she snapped, refusing to meet his eyes.

'Why's Hopkirk pursuing you?'

'I don't know!'

'I think you've a notion, though. I reckon you know a heap more than you're admitting.'

'No.'

Sam dropped his hands from her arms. 'All right. Just tell me this then, what made you collect these reports?'

'I didn't!' she protested shrilly. Her breasts heaved against the thin material of her shirt, parting it further at the open button, showing more of the cleavage between the ivory globes of her proud breasts.

'They were given me by Evan Gregg,' she went on. Her lips quivered. 'Pressed upon me, if you must know. He says he'll protect me, but I think he believes they'll let him . . . take liberties with me!'

Sam growled, 'Then he's a bigger scoundrel than I figured.'

'He says I should marry him one day.'

She paused, as though coming to a difficult decision, before plunging on with a torrent of surprising words.

'Not long since, after a dance in town, he got me alone outside in the dark, back of the hall. He gave me a rude kiss and thrust his hands up my clothes. He told me not to be a tease; he knew all good girls were whores at heart who longed to be deflowered, because hurtful though it might be they understood that once fairly got in working order, their transports henceforth would be complete. He was mortifyingly indelicate.'

'He must've been drunk.'

'I don't think so. His speech was as plain as it was vulgar. He talked like he proposed covering a heifer with a prize bull. He said the day was coming when he'd get inside me! There, you have the blunt horror of it in his very words! Now I think he believes the day has come. But I'd rather die than let him have his way.'

Red-faced, she turned her back on him.

Sam was also embarrassed by her outburst of frankness. Real Western men didn't speak to young ladies in the terms Gregg had used. Supposedly, it wasn't done . . . yet explicit journals and forbidden books and periodicals recording otherwise were printed privately — sometimes abroad as far away as Brussels or Amsterdam to avoid arrest on obscenity charges — and circulated in America discreetly.

'Look,' he said, 'this won't do. No decent feller would induce you to give in to him against your will. It ain't right. Your good mother being long passed, maybe you should talk to your pa. Or if that seems out of the question, I could have a careful word with him on your behalf, sparing details.'

She flared up again. 'It is out of the

question! For several good reasons that should be readily apparent.' Her tone calmed a fraction. 'To start with, he's away from home, I'm happy to say, and doesn't have to be bothered with any of this absurdity. Which also spares my feelings in the matter.'

A thought struck Sam. 'There's your aunt. Lorraine Delrose is Gregg's employer to boot.'

'I want nothing to do with that . . . that woman! She'd be the last person in whom I'd confide.'

Sam frowned. 'The cuttings must have some special significance, I guess. I'd like to know just how and why.'

'Stop it! I couldn't tell you! I don't know! It has to be a plot!' She choked as though with a sob. 'Now will you leave, Mr Hammond? Leave . . . please leave!'

'Very well.'

Sam could tell she was laden with despair and he knew of no way he could persuade or coerce her to explain further.

'I can see myself out. Just send me word in town if I can be of help.'

But Sam didn't mean to let it end there. And, as he passed outside by the window, going to his horse, his eye caught her dabbing her cheeks with a ridiculously small, lace-trimmed handkerchief.

She'd let flow the tears she'd held back. He knew she was supplying only the barest details of the truth.

What had he expected to hear? Was there some reasonable explanation behind the collection of cuttings and the denied unease they created? Gregg's tendering of them had evidently been accompanied by menaces and what might amount to no more than fantasies . . . of a dirty-minded, opportunist predator, intent on playing on girlish fears to accomplish the gratification of his lust.

What could he do to help Sarah Snyder?

6

Lorraine's Indiscretion

Draped with a white cloth and sitting in the padded, black leather customer chair, Sam Hammond looked out on the main street of Rainbow City as reflected in the big mirror of the barbershop. His jaw was well lathered with suds applied by a pig-bristle brush now back in the barber's mug.

All was calm outside and in, where the barber was industriously stropping his razor. His name was Albert Smith. A careful workman, he was proud of his razors and scissors and the edge he maintained on them. The sheriff was his most favoured customer. Smith appreciated that a public figure with a well-groomed moustache was in a measure a testament to and a walking advertisement for his tonsorial art.

When Sam had returned to town the previous day, he hadn't seen or heard anything more of Herb Hopkirk, so he presumed the stranger was behaving himself, while Evan Gregg, he supposed, had gone back to his work on the Triple S.

Maybe the fight out at the Diamond S was best forgotten.

He'd given thought to Clint Freeman, his injured deputy — whom he'd visited before taking the barber's chair — and to Sarah Snyder.

Clint was on the mend, though it was too soon to know whether his recovery would be complete or leave him with a limp.

Sarah Snyder was a more complex and puzzling matter. He didn't know whether further official investigation and intervention by himself was warranted; whether it would worsen her situation, whatever in truth that might be. He would have liked to alleviate the cause of her distress, just as he would have liked to ease Clint's physical discomfort.

But it was satisfying, a pure pleasure, that he'd sent the young miss's two tormentors, Hopkirk and Gregg, packing . . . if not exactly like scalded hounds, he'd dare say they'd been hounds with tails between their legs.

Finishing his stropping, Albert Smith said, 'Penny for your thoughts, Sam.'

Smith was a small man with a pigeon chest and sandy hair, mild-mannered, likeable and willing to indulge in agreeable patter, as befitted his occupation. He was also a good listener and sounding-board who could be counted on not to spread his customers' confidences as gossip.

Sam, thinking of Clint and Sarah one after the other, mumbled aloud and inconsequentially, 'They'd make a fine pair, Albert . . . my deputy and young Sarah Snyder.'

He stilled his lips as Smith applied the razor.

Smith said, 'Clint is a fine young feller and Miss Snyder is womenfolk of one of the county's best-placed families.'

'What do you make of Sarah Snyder?' Sam asked quickly as Smith paused to rinse the razor.

'Pretty as a picture. A jewel of a different kind to her aunt, Sam, for sure. Lorraine Delrose is a rule unto herself. Guess it comes of being a lady at one time on the stage. She's set the tongues wagging this time, by Gawd.'

'How d'you mean, Albert?'

He tugged his ear while he considered. 'Well, both customers before yourself today have carried on about it long and strong, so I guess it's public knowledge, notwithstanding you ain't heard yet.'

'Heard what?'

'Seems like La Delrose came into town late yesterday and dined with the shootist feller Hopkirk at the hotel.'

Sam frowned. 'I missed that, but what of it?'

Smith replied in tones a mite lower. 'Ain't so much a wonder you missed it,

Sam. Seems Hopkirk entertained her to supper in private — in his hotel room. She'd put up her buggy at the stable. And she didn't send for it and head back to her ranch till first light this morning. The hotel staff is tight-lipped, but the busybodies have been noising it about as a scandal since breakfast, maybe before.'

Sam was puzzled that Lorraine Delrose hadn't taken the opportunity to call on him. He wasn't surprised, however, that none of the few people he'd seen this morning had failed to mention the widow's perceived lapse from the commonly held standards of propriety. It was widely believed the former Mrs Snyder considered the sheriff her friend and that one day he might become more.

'I expect she must know Hopkirk somehow,' he suggested. 'A relative perhaps.'

Smith, who had a care not to voice judgements, shrugged. 'If she didn't know him, the talk is she probably does now.'

Sam said no more, but he speculated furiously. Lorraine was still a power in this land and he knew confirmation that she'd spent the night in Hopkirk's room would be hard to come by. Moreover, she was a widow-woman in her prime, in a position to lead her own life, and it was really none of his business what she did.

Two questions plagued him: was she aware of Hopkirk's unpleasantly ruthless character? How had their meeting come about? Was it in connection with the shooting of Lorraine's rider in the Gold Pot? Or was the motivation for the evident liaison dangerous dalliance of the kind he suspected Lorraine was craving to delight in?

Later, after pacing his office at several intervals between routine paperwork, he determined he was slightly beholden to the ranch-woman, if only in respect of the first-aid she'd given him after the show-down with the rustlers. He had a convincing duty to ride out to the Triple S, warn her about the range detective's true line of work and, without prying, learn the broad nature of their relationship if he could.

'Anything I can do to queer the gunhawk's pitch will be no chore,' he also admitted to himself.

He was continually mindful of how Hopkirk had gunned down Chelsum, what he had done to Clint Freeman, and his obnoxious interest in Sarah Snyder which rivalled Evan Gregg's.

★　★　★

As it happened, other business involving the disputed ownership of a horse delayed Sam and it was mid-afternoon before he was on the trail to the Triple S.

He passed Evan Gregg who was on his way into town. The foreman never seemed short of excuses for visiting Rainbow City and usually ended up calling at the Gold Pot.

It was on the tip of Sam's tongue to warn Gregg to keep clear of Herb Hopkirk, but he swiftly decided the range boss might respond with unhelpful antagonism, so he merely exchanged a curt 'howdy'. He arrived on the Triple S hot, dusty and sweaty, which didn't improve his mood as he slid from his saddle in front of the ranch house. He'd had plenty of time for feeling niggled that something was going on he hadn't known about.

Lorraine saw him from a window and quickly opened the door to come out on to her grand porch.

'Sam!' she exclaimed, her shining eyes wide. 'How nice to see you. Why have you come out here?'

She was wearing a practical blouse and skirt, but was perpetually the classic, fuller-figured beauty, not over-large albeit well-developed in the bosom as might be expected of a former professional singer. The thin stuff of the red blouse did little to conceal her generous assets.

Lorraine's vivid presence tended to discompose timid men, but not Sam.

'I came to hear from your own lips

what happened last night in town,' Sam said. 'Not the tittle-tattle, but the facts, Lorraine. Understand?'

'Why, I don't know that I do. Unless it's that you're jealous . . . ' She laughed at his stern face. 'How delightful! I always knew it was going to happen some day — you were going to see things my way. Want to feel your body touching mine. Is it too late for a bath and a little siesta after your hot ride? I could wash your back and my bed is still waiting for you to share. What do you think?'

Sam knew she was winding him up.

'You've less damn shame than Jenny Abernethy's girls! That's what I think. Haven't you a ranch — a business — to run?'

'Sadly, yes . . . and all too little time to spare on teasing you. Come on in.'

Inside, she offered him a drink.

'Lemonade would be acceptable,' he said. 'I have the ride back. Hot sun and strong liquor don't mix.'

'More's the pity,' she said, and

poured him a glass. 'Liquor might make you more . . . sociable.'

There was depth to her, frankness and a quickness of mind that appealed, though the flip side of the coin was that a cautious man might never be able to relax his guard with her. She could, and would, manipulate without restraint or compunction. If ever she gave an impression she was dumb or helpless, it was because that was the way she chose to play it.

'Did you know it was Hopkirk who shot dead your rider Chelsum?' he prodded.

Her eyes met his, cool and defiant. Again, she had nettling amusement in her voice.

'Evan Gregg told me. That cow-hand was of little use to the Triple S. Less brain than the cattle he was hired to help run. Good only for underestimating things — and people like Herb Hopkirk.'

A fly buzzed lazily against a window-pane while Sam framed his next question, keeping calm.

'So what are you doing, consorting with Hopkirk?' he asked into the hot stillness.

She laughed outright, her eyes sparkling, taunting. 'I think you *must* be jealous! Consorting . . . '

'Oh, damnit! Stop the funning and answer the question, can't you? He's a vicious, dangerous man. Why were you in his room?'

She looked at him with a change to calculation in her eyes.

'It was my idea, I suppose. We needed to talk privately — only talk.'

'About what?'

'About Dick Slick.'

That name again! Sam was rocked back on his heels. Why were the two most beautiful females in the district interested in a hold-up artist? Not any outlaw — such, after all, did exercise fascination over some women's glamorizing imaginations — but the very same one?

'Dick Slick is the handle writers for the sensationalist press have given a bank robber,' he said. 'How would such a character figure in conversation between a Concho County rancher and a hard-headed range detective? It doesn't add up.'

She let her mouth curve again in a rueful smile.

'Oh, Sam! There's a lot you don't know about women!' A huskiness came into her voice. 'It's another of their pesky indispositions, I guess . . . Most gals find a rich and successful man a subject of interest, whatever he does to make his fortune.'

And romance clung to the lawless, Sam thought, regardless that they were for the larger part scum, dirty and shiftless, without principles or decency, sometimes habitual drunks. The West was made for the criminals and the plain cheats — a place for a man to disappear down the owlhoot trails; into vast and trackless wilderness. Sam's comfort was that it also ultimately destroyed many of them, while the strong and hardworking could, with any sort of luck, survive and in due course prosper.

Unconvinced by Lorraine's explanation, which was flimsy for a woman of her maturity and background, he fired another question.

'Did you know your niece Sarah Snyder had a collection of newspaper cuttings about this same Dick Slick — that she says your foreman gave 'em her?'

Lorraine's quick intake of breath was instantly suppressed.

'Ah, so that's what he did with them!' she said, her eyes glittering brightly. 'The cuttings were mine.'

Possibly it was no remarkable admission. She'd said she'd met with Hopkirk to discuss the bank robber. Sam also suddenly remembered where and when he'd seen the tape that had tied the bundle: a reel of it had been in Lorraine's rolltop desk after his punishing gunfight with the rustlers.

She sighed, then scoffed. 'What a fool Evan Gregg is! Did you know he nurses a ridiculous notion he might better his station in life by impressing young Sarah and winning her as his bride?'

'I'd heard some such. It don't sound reasonable.'

'It's stupid for a man his age!'

'I can savvy he's too old for the filly.'

'Mr Gregg has a high opinion of his — vigour. After Rex died he made advances to me, trying to make progress for himself by getting in my good graces, I guess . . .'

Sam reflected silently that Lorraine seemed to have spent a lifetime consciously or contrariwise inveigling all men to dance to her pretty tune.

'Howsoever. I let it be known to the worm that I'd read what was in his mind — his thoughts were obvious — and I didn't reciprocate his lust.'

'That must have been an awkward scene.'

'Not for me — for Evan Gregg. When I'd finished my little speech of deli-cately chosen words, he was burning red. Not with embarrassment but with hate for himself, consumed as he was by desires too big for the body they were locked within and that could never, ever be consummated. Gregg was put in his place as foreman of the Triple S. That and no more.'

Sam rubbed his chin. 'It'd be enough for many men. Maybe he should be content with his lot here.'

'But of course he's not,' Lorraine continued, and carried away by her frankness and Sam's absorption revealed yet more.

'The Diamond S will one day be Sarah's, and it's in better shape than my property can ever be. Like most hereabout, this outfit is mortgaged to the hilt to the Rainbow City bank.'

Sam was puzzled. 'But you've been doing fair. You bought a few graded Durham bulls last year, and they were a good buy. They'll increase the weight of your critters year after year. That'll pay off in the long haul, fetching you top prices.'

She gave him a look he could only call sheepish.

'I bought the graded bulls with money loaned me open-ended by Sarah's father. Does that surprise you?' She laughed derisively. 'My dear brother-in-law is another fool! Thinks I might marry him and he'll get his hands on the Triple S. Make the ranches one again.'

'Would that be so bad?' Sam asked. He knew full well Lorraine would admire to put her brand on himself, but he was too aware of the downside of falling into her toils.

She answered him indirectly. 'I know John Snyder of old. Very well. I'll say only that nothing's so bad for a woman as a man who thinks he's good. I prefer a man I find exciting . . . '

Sam frowned. He was uncomfortable with the direction Lorraine was trying again to steer his visit.

'All right, but I came here to talk about something else, and you know it. Herb Hopkirk, Dick Slick — I aim to get to the bottom of this boiling — '

He got no further. A rider pounded

into the yard outside, reined in to a slithering halt, dropped from the saddle and sprang up the porch steps. It was the boy from the livery barn in Rainbow.

'Sheriff! Mr Hammond, sir! You better ride back t' town pronto, Sheriff! All hell's about t' bust loose!'

7

Stairway to Hell?

The boy was wide-eyed and breathless with excitement, eager to tell his important story.

'I tol' Deputy Clint at the doc's an' he said to ride real fast an' git yuh, Mr Hammond. Whole town's talkin' 'bout nothin' else!'

Sam said tensely, between his teeth, 'Come to the urgent part, kid. What the hell's happened?'

'Seems like the salty stranger that shot Clint got in a yellin' ruckus with a lady in the street. Then he plumb forced her to go with 'im back inta the hotel an' took her upstairs t' his room. The sonofabitch!'

On the minute, Sam knew there was something much worse afoot than he'd suspected. His eyes went slaty.

'The lady — was it Sarah Snyder?'

'Yeah, that's who it was, sure 'nough.'

Sam figured it out. With his deputy laid up and himself ridden out of town, Hopkirk had seized his chance to put renewed pressure on Sarah.

'So what're the townfolks doing?'

'Nothin' much, I guess. They're plumb scairt. Ever'body seen he's gotten a gun-hand like hot hell. It ain't right, is it?'

'You can be damn sure it's not! Not by a long sight!'

'But that ain't all. Evan Gregg was in the Gold Pot. When they tol' 'im, he said they was yeller-gutted sons as didn't have enough sand in their craws to help a gal in trouble. He went to the hotel, but the man up thar — '

'Hopkirk.'

'Yeah, Hopkirk . . . he wouldn't let the gal come down. Said he was a-holdin' her till he'd gotten answers.'

'So then what?'

'Evan Gregg was a-carryin' on in the street under Hopkirk's winder. He was callin' 'im out for a gun duel on Main Street in an hour when I lit out o' town lickety-spit!'

Sam needed to hear no more. He and his informant set out hell bent for leather for Rainbow City.

The mad journey offered no chance for further questions and, his horse being the longer rested and the more powerfully built, Sam quickly drew ahead. A vision of young Sarah, naked from the pool, swam before him.

Deliberately, he pushed thought of her captivity — if that was what it was — out of his mind. He remembered how she'd refused to tell all she knew and asked him to leave the Diamond S, shunning his help. He wondered if she still felt the same way.

A scant hour later, he thundered into Rainbow City, every echoing hoofbeat of his blood-bay gelding bringing him the last steps closer to the hotel and a showdown with the nasty, dangerous piece of work that was Herb Hopkirk.

The hotel was on the opposite side of

the street from the Gold Pot. A group of men stood outside the saloon, their eyes on the other place, one empty upstairs window in particular.

Among them was Evan Gregg.

He bulled forward aggressively as Sam reined in. He was beside himself with fury.

'So yuh come back, huh? So much for your hard words to me an' Hopkirk! The sidewinder's got Sarah up in his room. If she ain't outa there in ten minutes when the bar clock chimes, I'm gonna go in an' smash his goddamn door down. What the hell does he think he's playin' at?'

A voice chipped in, 'They say the dirty son had that hot opera-singer woman sleepin' over last night. You know what he's playin' at. Some men e'n never git enough an' help theirselves fer free.'

'Disgusting!' a woman said.

'Seems to me it's mebbe only as disgustin' as some little misses ask for.'

Gregg roared, 'I can't wait no more!

106

I'll surely kill 'im!'

Sam said, 'Shuddup, the lot of you!' He jumped in front of Gregg as he started toward the hotel.

'Hold it, Gregg! Get a grip on yourself, man. The idiots know nothing. They're riling you up with crazy windies for the hell of it.'

But Gregg shoved a calloused hand in his face. 'Outa my way, yuh useless ol' lawdog!'

Sam was hurled aside on feet still unsteady from his hard ride, but he kept his balance. Gregg's temper and the damnfool horseplay of the saloon's front-door 'punchers were going to get him killed.

'Hey, come back!' he yelled. 'Hopkirk's a seasoned shootist. You're asking to get killed going up against him!'

Had Gregg forgotten what had happened to Chelsum? Hopkirk had blown out his lamp. To Clint Freeman? Hopkirk had left him nearly crippled.

He drew his six-gun and span it so the barrel landed in the palm of his hand. Well, if he won't pull in his horns, it'll be for his own good, he thought.

He loped after Gregg; went up the four steps into the hotel two at a time. It was no situation for kid-glove handling. He'd be doing Gregg a kindness. Catching up with him halfway across the lobby to the stairs, he slammed the hard butt of the gun against the side of the man's head.

Gregg stumbled and fell. He went down like a man meeting his shadow. His face smacked into the polished floorboards and a single, breathy moan burst from his lips. He was out cold.

Sam went on to the foot of the stairs. Whatever Hopkirk was doing up there, he must have heard the crash of Gregg's fall. It had shaken the building.

'All right, Hopkirk!' he shouted. 'The game's gone far enough. Folks want to see you and Miss Snyder both, down here at the front desk. Pronto!'

Scuffling sounds and a small, female cry reached his ears. The door to Hopkirk's room was opening.

'Stay put, kid, just as you are, and you won't get hurt,' the range dick's harsh voice said. Then Hopkirk appeared alone and slammed the door shut behind him.

To his dismay, Sam saw he was in shirtsleeves and wearing a belt gun. He was ready for trouble, heeled for a fight.

'Seems like you taken to kidnapping now, Hopkirk,' Sam said. 'Locking up a nice girl in your room.'

Hopkirk stopped on the stairs. 'You're going off half-cocked, Sheriff. Misreading the facts on the say-so of a hotheaded cow-nurse. We're continuing a little interrupted talk, is all.'

'No one likes the idea of a young lady being held prisoner. That's carrying things too far.'

To Sam's shock, Hopkirk suddenly went into a gunman's crouch and made a snatching draw. Sam was caught flat-footed. He figured it was all up for him. He was about to be gunned down in a shoot-out he hadn't picked, on account of a quarrel that wasn't of his making and had spiralled way out of hand.

It was the gunfight that was one too many.

He started to go for his own gun.

Hopkirk fired.

The slug zipped past Sam a split-second before a second gun blasted behind him and a white torrent of smashed plaster fell from the ceiling.

God almighty! Was he going to get backshot, too?

If a man had a choice between standing still and getting killed and moving and getting killed, Sam knew which he preferred.

He flung himself away from the stairs and vaulted over a bulky sofa. Gun drawn, he peered round it, assessing what the hell was going on.

Sam should have known. If Hopkirk had meant to kill him — Sam Hammond — he could have. At such short range, he could have shot out the pips on a playing card.

Through the reeking swirls of gun-smoke and the settling cloud of ceiling plaster, the real story became visibly apparent.

Evan Gregg had a thicker skull than Sam had judged. Recovering consciousness on the floor behind Sam, Gregg had lifted his pained head to see his supposed rival for the virtue of Sarah Snyder looming on the stairs. Though dazed, he'd gone for his gun and suffered the dire consequences. A smoking pistol was still in his hand. Blood was on his vest and trickled from the corner of his mouth.

'Gawd!' one of the bystanders breathed. 'Gregg's dyin'!'

Hopkirk snapped, 'Aw, damnit! Yeah — I've settled the locoed old beau's hash! The has-been buckaroo drew a gun and purely got what was coming to him.'

'Some epitaph,' someone grunted. 'Unworthier fellers've won better.'

Hopkirk hooked his fingers belligerently in his belt. 'As a man once observed, dying ain't a difficult task,' he said coldly. 'All you have to be is alive and a mite stupid.'

Sam went to Gregg's side, dropping to his knees, though he knew there'd be nothing he could for him.

The optimistic were calling for the doc.

Gregg was losing consciousness again, but he strived to lift his head. The words he tried to utter were those of a man in delirium.

' . . . Dick Slick . . . Sarah's . . . the bounty! Sh-she'll do 'bout anything for — '

'Who? Sarah? Do what?'

In the growing hubbub of consternation, Gregg's voice was rasping, increasingly faint, complete words inaudible. Soon it was no more than ragged breathing, bubbling through the frothy blood from his lungs.

All at once, as Gregg slumped back glassy-eyed and it seemed like the scene around him was freezing into a tableau respecting the presence of death, everything dissolved into fresh confusion.

Above, the door to Hopkirk's room burst open and Sarah Snyder appeared at the head of the stairs, looking dishevelled and distressed but still fully dressed in bonnet and smart street clothes. She paused, her face blanching with horror.

'Oh, God!' she cried, and came down the stairs in a rush, sobbing.

But Hopkirk grabbed her as she tried to pass him. His gun was out of the holster again and he wrapped his arm around her neck.

'I told you to stay where you were!' he snarled. He was plainly angered afresh that he'd been ignored.

She screamed and he jammed the muzzle of the gun into her side.

'All right — so be it!' Hopkirk said, addressing those who'd dared to enter the lobby. He started the rest of the way down the stairs.

The girl was helpless to resist him though her hands scrabbled at his strong arm. Fear and a look of resignation came over her face, masking

113

its prettiness with something almost ugly.

She was dragged and pushed, held up by him as she stumbled down each step.

Hopkirk, though, didn't make one that was false. His voice took on a shrillness. He was giving the orders and God help any gritty bastard who dared defy him.

'Stand back, you hicks, or she gets it in the guts! We're leaving for quieter places. And the man that tries to stop us will be the second one to die!'

Using Sarah as his shield and hostage, he backed to the door.

Sam said, 'You can't get away with this for ever, sonofabitch!'

But though he spoke with all the conviction he could muster, he knew it would be one hell of an impossible job to save Sarah Snyder from whatever Hopkirk had in mind for her.

If anyone acted rashly, her death would be quick and certain.

8

Lost Tracks

Herb Hopkirk pushed Sarah Snyder at gunpoint across the street. He told her to climb into her buggy, which still stood at rest, the patient horses half-dozing, their tails switching. He jumped up after her.

'Hit the road, gal! We're leaving town, but fast. Whip up those fine high-steppers like the Devil's on their tails!'

'The Devil is right beside me,' Sarah jerked.

The expression that came to Hopkirk's face would have made a stone madonna weep for mercy.

'You getting any notion in your head to oppose me, I'll knock it out again. Do as you're told!'

The matching pair squealed as Sarah

reluctantly, fearfully put them into rapid motion.

Sam Hammond was baffled by the turn of events.

A bullet came from the buggy as it hurtled off down the street, beginning its wild dash out of Rainbow City, its red-spoked wheels a blur. It was a warning bullet, aimed no place in particular, as though Hopkirk was merely letting the gawking citizenry know he was serious.

It served its purpose.

These people were merchants, traders, pig farmers, the storekeepers' wives and daughters, Jenny Abernethy's painted, tittering whores, some cowmen. They had little stomach or ability for chasing a madman with a quick gun and a girl who might have asked for trouble. No one ventured to ride after the disappearing cloud of swirling dust.

And it took Sam a full half-hour before he could put together a posse.

'He's abducted an innocent young woman,' he heard himself plead in protest, though it was growing no easier for him to figure out the motive for this.

What part did Sarah Snyder play in the unravelling events? She'd earlier resisted telling him all she knew, he was certain-sure; refused his help and sent him away from the Diamond S, his curiosity about several matters unsatisfied.

He finally deputized four men prepared to ride out with him in pursuit, though Carter, Blake, Chester and Colwyn had no relish for the job. His mind planned what had to be done, dividing the territory into sections, listing likely places for Hopkirk to flee with his prisoner; places where he might wrest from her the answers he wanted and which it seemed she wanted to give no one on any terms. He was daunted on realizing even a short list was long.

How long would Sarah hold out once Hopkirk had her away from what passed for civilization and he began — in total, undisturbed privacy — to do the things a vicious, ruthless man might do to a young woman to make her bend to his will?

The first blow to the chase was losing the buggy's tracks. They were difficult enough to differentiate on the well-used stage road running south from the town. When they left the route and went down into one of the district's many dry creek beds, the followers were stumped. It was impossible to figure whether the buggy was driven across the creek, or went along its trough over smooth, hard boulders.

Sam spent a half-hour checking the ground round about. Other tracks showed that the creek bed had been used as a cut-off countless times, probably because it offered a saving in time over the conventional route. And the tracks left the course of the absent creek every which way.

Who had made what tracks? Baffled, Sam swore.

The full blast of the afternoon sun made the task no easier, and he pushed his posse to the limit, breaking it into pairs, searching the slopes for signs of promising, recent making.

The four men grew hotter, and testy. They were not the best of trackers and Sam could do only so much himself.

'There's trails, but any or all of 'em could be false, Mr Hammond,' Chester said. 'We'll be wastin' our time tryin' to foller each. It's madness . . . '

Colwyn added, 'We'll be goin' back to town not jest empty-handed, but plumb tuckered out.'

Blake raised his hat and scratched his head. 'I reck'n we been given a bum steer.'

Carter said, 'I don't want be made to look a fool.'

'Yeah . . . ' Sam gritted, holding his temper in check. 'And you don't want to wind up dead either.'

They were affronted.

'We're no cowards, Sheriff, if that's what you're suggestin',' Colwyn said, speaking bluntly for all the possemen, 'but they could be anyplace . . . Must have a good hour on us now, an' still travellin'. Mebbe more'n five mile away.'

Chester said, 'That far, easy.'

In frustration, Sam rapped, 'Then we gotta make up the time fast!'

'An' mebbe look double-damned fools if he's holed up close in some hidey-hole,' Blake opined.

'Then we find the hidey-hole!'

'How?' Colwyn asked in reasonable tones. 'We ain't got the manpower when it could be one of a hundr'd places, Sam. Hopkirk was in his rights to kill Gregg, as much as he was killin' Chelsum. What're we out here for? To defend a woman's honour? Seems to me Snyder's daughter's turnin' out a brat an' a troublemaker.'

Sam's gorge rose, but he had to swallow it.

He thought he recognized Sarah Snyder for what she was: a girl who'd lived a privileged, relatively sheltered life and who was in trouble. But his possemen didn't have that understanding. Many of the unmarried women around Rainbow City, if they weren't born in the district, came out of saloons, dance halls or worse. How else could they have worked their passage this far west? So what his possemen saw in Sarah's plight was distorted by prejudice and cynicism. Independent women spelled trouble, got what they asked for.

It went against the grain to call off the search, but Sam did. 'All right, we're wasting time, I guess. I'll have to try something else.'

'Beats me what there is left to try,' Colwyn said wearily.

'I'm thinking about checking out with Lorraine Delrose.'

'Why?'

'She — she spent time with Hopkirk. I'll get back and speak with her some more about it. Hopkirk may have let something slip.'

The possemen brightened.

'Suit yourself.'

'Ain't no sense in us traipsin' all over the country.'

'Sounds reasonable to me.'

'If La Delrose'll level with anyone, it'll be you, Sam. She's another rich bitch with a mind of her own.'

Sam's face, like everybody's, was too hot to flush any more.

★　★　★

Sam felt awful tired. He was tired from the unsuccessful, aborted pursuit of Hopkirk. He was tired of what was threatening to turn into a spate of shooting and killing in his quiet town.

Maybe he really should think seriously about handing in his badge once he'd cleaned up the mess created since Hopkirk's arrival.

Particularly, he was tired of being lied to by scheming women who knew more than they would let on . . .

It was coming dark when he reached the Triple S on a fresh mount. Lamps blazed in the front rooms of Lorraine's fine ranch house, but he noted this time, maybe from a trick of more dismal light, that the outfit was starting to look run down. A gate sagged on its hinges, considerable whitewash would be needed to return certain buildings to peak condition, and some shakes were missing from the roof of the largely unoccupied bunkhouse.

Dismounting and loosening a saddle girth, Sam didn't look forward to crossing verbal swords with the autocratic widow who was mistress of all he surveyed.

She answered his quiet knock herself, and her playful manner quickly made evident that she hadn't heard yet about the death of her foreman in Rainbow City.

'Why, if it isn't Sheriff Hammond again!' Lorraine greeted him teasingly. 'Maybe somebody, somewhere might be hankering to know what he's been missing nights . . . '

Sam didn't bite. At the moment, he was more interested in finding Hopkirk and stuffing him down into the muck beneath the nearest and fullest privy he could find.

'I came to pick up with the line of questions I was asking before I was called back to town.'

Lorraine pulled a petulant face. 'Oh, Sam, must you be so dull!'

Gravel-voiced, he said, 'Dull or not, it's part of my work as sheriff to make such enquiries.'

'Meanwhile, what am I supposed to do when the working day is over? It comes next to insult to have a fine, upstanding *hombre* refusing to join me in bed.'

In the privacy they shared, Sam couldn't tell how much of what she was saying was serious and how much amounted to prodding him into a reaction for fun. But because he was alone with her, least of all was he embarrassed.

He cut fast and without shilly-shally to important matters. He scored immediately.

'The Triple S has lost its foreman,

Lorraine. Evan Gregg was shot dead today in Rainbow City . . . by Herb Hopkirk.'

Lorraine was startled. The smile vanished. Colour drained from her face.

'Good God! Did you let the idiots shoot it out? I realized Gregg wasn't back, of course. I thought maybe you'd locked him up for disturbing the peace.'

Sam told how he'd arrived in time to prevent the threatened gun duel, but how shots had been exchanged in the hotel lobby anyway.

Lorraine had no grief for Gregg, or she kept herself so completely under control that she didn't betray any emotion. A heavy silence settled in the room, till she broke the brief calm with an exclamation of annoyance.

'Blast it! This puts me at an awkward disadvantage. Knowing the worst is knowing where you stand, that's for sure. The Triple S happened to rely heavily on Gregg for its day-to-day running. I don't make a habit of working cattle.'

A shadow of worry appeared in her eyes, and Sam was sure this time she wasn't acting. He sighed.

'Be that as maybe, there are priorities other than your property's manning, Lorraine. Hopkirk has abducted Sarah Snyder. Spirited her away. Ridden off with her God knows where . . . and maybe your ownself.'

Lorraine dropped her gaze secretively and trailed fingers over the deep polish of a solid mahogany sideboard.

'Yes, I might, mightn't I?'

'You have a duty to tell then. What do you know about Hopkirk's business here? Where does the stuff about Dick Slick fit in? It's high time you came clean, Lorraine. I don't trust that so-called range detective with your young niece.'

Abruptly, the wavering woman said, 'Herb Hopkirk was engaged by myself, for his professional services.'

Sam was surprised and did nothing not to let it show.

'You hired a detective? I thought you

were short of cash-money.'

'I put it on the slate, you might say.' Her tone took on assurance. 'The arrangement was we'd share the reward money for Dick Slick fifty-fifty. I'd supply the information that would make it possible to unmask the bank robber and claim the three thousand dollars for his capture.'

Sam's head reeled.

'You summoned Hopkirk in his occupation as a bounty hunter? You know who Dick Slick is? That he's *here*, someplace around Rainbow?'

Lorraine's eyes flared with self-congratulation. Triumphantly, she answered, 'Yes, yes, and yes!'

9

Sarah is Rash

Around the same time Sam Hammond was riding to the Triple S homeplace for the second time in a day, Sarah Snyder was bringing her buggy to a standstill before a line-camp on the northern-most edge of the Triple S.

It was a gloomy scene: a twenty-by-twenty shack, whose weather-greyed siding had long since not benefited from paint, and a broken-poled corral huddled in shifting purple shadows under a dark, browning green canopy of hoary old oaks.

Sarah knew the old place vaguely. It had been abandoned and the roof leaked like a sieve, but local swains sometimes brought girls out here who should have known better than to trust in it as a bower for pleasurable experiences. Isolated and offering only the most primitive comforts, it was unfit, unworthy for any honest use.

She viewed the tumbledown building with disgust, her nose wrinkling.

Herb Hopkirk said drily, 'It's a wonder what holds the place up, but it'll serve.'

'Why have you made me drive here?' Sarah demanded, dropping the reins.

Herb Hopkirk leered at her evilly. 'Best damn buggy ride I've had in a coon's age.'

'That isn't true,' she said weakly.

'Maybe the arriving will be better than the travelling.'

'What do you mean?'

'Here is a whole lot better than pussyfooting around with you in a comfortable hotel in town. You saw what that brought down. At this dump, I get to make you tell me what I want to know without interference. Who's going to hear a few screams in the empty hills?'

'I told you!' Sarah shrilled. 'I know

nothing! This is outrageous!'

Hopkirk jumped out of the buggy. 'Come on, get down!' he ordered, reaching up for her arm. 'Way you've been acting, you've asked for a damn good paddling and more! There'll be tears besides information before I've finished.'

For an instant, Sarah was paralysed with fright. She felt desolation — her own deepened by the atmosphere of the grim surroundings — like a hard knot in her belly.

'Out, I say!' Hopkirk snapped, the set of his scarred face turning impatient.

'You daren't hurt me,' she said in a trembling voice.

Hopkirk laughed, deep in his throat, without humour. 'Daren't I? What it amounts to is I do howsoever I like. Telling stories will only do you extra harm, since we'll make 'em ones few will want to believe. I think I'm going to enjoy this. Under the circumstances, you'd have to agree it'd be impossible for any hot-blooded male to be — uh

— dispassionate.'

Aghast as she was at his threat, she dredged up the last reserves of spirit. Feeling giddy, it wasn't hard for her to reel as she stood up. Could she pluck up the courage to defy him? She had a premonition she was faced with her last chance. Once he got her into the shack, he'd do horrible, unspeakable things as he'd intimated. Make her tell her secrets . . .

With unpredictable abruptness, she threw her full weight at him, knocking him from his feet. She almost lost her own balance, too. The impact knocked the breath out of her body.

But somehow she ran. She gulped air into her lungs and her legs pumped beneath her.

Hopkirk bellowed, *'Bitch! That does it!'*

He scrambled up and plunged after her, in no way incapacitated by the fall, maybe less winded than she'd been herself.

He rapidly gained on her as she sped

131

through the trees, twisting and turning. It was hopeless. Far from any settlement, she had nowhere to run for safety.

The final, decidedly crushing blow to her desperate bid for freedom was an exposed root in her path. She didn't see it until it was too late. Her foot tripped and her legs quit smooth working. She staggered on a few more paces, momentum carrying her forward, hands outflung, before going down, face first, sprawling full-length.

Her head struck a rock.

★　★　★

Lorraine Delrose was ready to sing as she'd never sung before. Sam thought it was possible she was more put out by the loss of Evan Gregg's services than she'd said.

'Hopkirk went too far!' she said in consternation. 'Do you think he plans to double-cross me?'

'I don't know what he plans, or what

you'd planned with him.'

He took her firmly by the upper arms and made her face him. He spoke sternly.

'You haven't been frank, and now I need to know the truth — all of it before there's more shooting and killing.'

'I said . . . I hired Hopkirk as a kind of — partner. His experience and muscle, my knowledge.'

'It sounds crazy, fantastic! Your knowledge being that you know the identity of Dick Slick?'

'I think so.'

Sam put the key question. 'Who?'

Lorraine summoned the vestiges of her regal manner.

'I'm surprised that it isn't blindingly obvious to you, Sam, what with John Snyder's frequent absences and Hopkirk's pestering of his daughter . . . which wasn't my idea, incidentally.'

Sam fought to control his reaction to what she was claiming. It did fit with facts, but nonetheless, her contention came hard for him to believe, though he couldn't say he didn't believe it.

'John Snyder is Dick Slick? A bank robber?'

'That's what I'm saying, isn't it?' she said crossly.

'How did you find out?'

She laughed, though not nicely. 'Well, he didn't tell me!'

'But you will me,' Sam insisted. 'What makes you so certain? Have you proof of any sort?'

Lorraine remained silent for a moment, then she said, 'I *know* him and I had suspicions for ages. But what put me on the track in earnest was the wound.'

Sam frowned. 'I didn't know about that.'

'Of course not. You aren't his sister-in-law. He kept it dark. Very dark.'

Sam reviewed what he did know himself. John Snyder was often away from the successful Diamond S, putting his trips down to business and a liking for city lights formed in younger days when his powerful father was still in the world and he and his brother, Rex, led lives and developed tastes that only the sons of wealthy families could afford.

'Explain what you know about this wound,' Sam asked.

'John was always vague about his time away, but he came back once with a nasty bullet wound in his side. He told me he'd been in Sacramento and a man had tried to hold him up for his wallet. He'd driven the fellow off but was wounded in the fight.'

'Believable.'

'Yet the wound was at least a week old, infected, inflamed and giving him a lot of trouble. He hadn't sought professional attention — that much was apparent.'

'And what did you do when you found out?'

Lorraine shrugged. 'I told him he should've already seen a doctor and should see one then. He refused. He insisted Sarah could tend to it — dress it and so forth — and that he didn't have time to be running backwards and forwards to the sawbones in Rainbow City. Nor would he waste his money, or the man's time, in requesting house calls. He was adamant he wanted no fuss.'

Sam still didn't see that Snyder was damned by the incident.

'It could have happened exactly as he said, surely.'

'But like as not it didn't!' she snapped. 'The date coincided exactly with that of a botched bank robbery by the Dick Slick gang in Sacramento. Shots were fired. It was reported in the newspapers.'

The significance of the collection of cuttings, and Sarah's consternation about them, dawned on Sam.

'You think John Snyder has been living a double life?'

'I'm sure of it. He has better grazing country than the Triple S, but I know he, too, was on the verge of losing his ranch to the bank when the bad seasons ate into our stock and money reserves. Every time, he managed to come up on time with the necessary funds for his mortgage payments. He has also helped me, putting up the money for the graded Durham bulls as a virtual gift, interest free. Why, next season, he wants me to introduce Aberdeen Angus and Shorthorns. He figures if we breed from a cross of both of them we'll have the finest cattle south of the Bozeman Trail.'

Sam nodded. 'The polled, black Aberdeen Angus give you heavy beef sure enough. Ambitious. You agree with him?'

Lorraine raised her chin. 'In point of fact, no. I accepted his largesse last time against my better judgement. You know I hate to be beholden to anyone. Like I already told you, he was angling to amalgamate our holdings through marriage. It wouldn't work!'

'Maybe you're letting your prejudice in that matter colour your thoughts, making you suspicious of your late husband's brother.'

Sam made the suggestion gently,

reasonably, he thought, but Lorraine flared up.

'How much more evidence does it take to convince a cloth-headed sheriff!'

'Enough to persuade a jury maybe.'

'Very well! Consider this: there was another newspaper story about a distinctive timepiece, perfectly described by the writer as an English gold hunter watch. It belonged to a bank manager in Red Bluff, given him by the bank for twenty-five years' loyal service. John Snyder, alias Dick Slick, took it along with the contents of the bank's safe.'

Sam frowned in puzzlement. 'How do you know this?'

'Because I saw it! One day on John Snyder's desk.' Lorraine allowed herself a complacent smile, sure of her facts. 'Before I could touch it and examine some engraving on its cover, John whisked it into his pocket. I asked about it, saying something admiring, but he brushed me off, saying it had belonged to his father.'

'There you have it then,' Sam said.

'An innocent explanation.'

'No! Old man Snyder left all his personal items to his eldest son. My husband Rex inherited the lot, all the little gew-gaws. Only the real estate was divided.'

Lorraine's smile was gloating. When it came to argument she was always the one who had the last, winning word.

★   ★   ★

Sarah's head rang. She had an awareness of rough hands seizing her arms, bruising the soft flesh. She moaned and another wave of blackness washed over her. The next vague feeling she had was of being lifted and carried.

Something slapped her face — hard. Slapped again. And again. 'D-don't . . . ' she slurred. She forced her head to rise, her eyes to open.

As fuller consciousness returned, she found herself staring straight into Herb Hopkirk's face. She flinched at its hardness, the ugliness of the scar, and the burning intensity in his eyes. Her tongue felt thick and useless in her mouth.

'Well, aren't you going to ask where you are?' he jeered.

Hugely frightened, she stared around and tried to shrink back.

'I know where I am.'

She was in the horrible shack at the Triple S's deserted line-camp, the prisoner of a man with demands, and maybe designs, that filled her with trepidation.

Clearest of all was the knowledge she mustn't give in. She was strong for a girl and healthy, and she would have to try until the very last to break free. Again, she pluckily made a decision and, without warning, launched herself at Hopkirk.

This time she ripped his face with her fingernails.

His head whipped back, red scores on his mudpale nose and cheek.

He swore, and grappled to restrain her.

Sarah knew a thing or two about rough-and-tumble, having on the odd occasion witnessed fights between cowhands, a rugged breed not known for pansy ways. She brought up her knee, forcefully.

He grunted, cussed again filthily, and called her a hell-cat. Soon, he held her easily. He was a powerful man. She squirmed in his hands.

'I do admire a gal with spirit!' he grated.

Though it was futile, Sarah pummelled ineffectively with her tight fists. Hopkirk's eyes gleamed.

'Shit,' he said thickly, 'you sure are a little spitfire.'

He cracked a fist to her chin and she was thrown back, stunned a second time.

She came to her senses to find she was lying on a malodorous palliasse. Her wrists and ankles were tied to the shack's single, rusted iron bedstead. Bits of hard straw poked and scratched wherever her skin was bare on arms and legs. Fear clutched at her heart.

'Want to play it tough, huh?' he said. He drew a knife from a sheath hidden at the back of his waistband. 'You know what I've got, or rather your knee does. Now let's see what you got.'

Her cheeks flushed, and the folds of her loose-fitting blouse rose and fell at the bosom in time with her quick breathing. Her eyes glazed with impotent horror as he brought the glittering blade closer. She'd never known such total terror.

He put the point of the knife to her throat and suddenly ripped downwards, severing her clothes to the waist. She let loose a piercing scream, but when she tried to scream again only a wild, hysterical sobbing came from her lips.

He flicked the flaps of cut, delicate garments to either side with the knife-tip and looked at her, nude from the waist up, as though contemplating the features of her anatomy where he might next apply the sharp blade.

A stinging red scratch ran down her lightly tanned front. Here and there she was sure it was beaded with blood where the indiscriminate knife had broken the skin as well as severed fabric.

'Remember, it was your idea it should be this way. Circumstances compel, seeing as how you refused to tell me civilly all I have to know. Like a well-behaved miss. Unless you talk, it's only going to get worse for you. You get my meaning?' He touched the point of the knife to a nipple. 'If a few nicks here and there ain't enough . . . well, maybe we can pull down your skirt and drawers and start over someplace else . . . '

He broke off and chuckled. 'Might do that anyhow.'

★   ★   ★

With the girl's eyes wide with terror, her beauty provoked in Hopkirk more than a mild thrill. Maybe it was no bad thing she'd resisted him. She was a sweeter piece of womanflesh than he'd had in a long while.

Possession, persuasion, profit . . . he could see it all lined up and unfolding.

10

You're Under Arrest!

Sam was staggered by Lorraine's smug confidence. The evidence of the stolen watch would be damning for sure, if it could be produced. He felt she was secretly laughing at him, playing him for a complete sucker, assuming she had only to tell her story to win him to her side and her will. His pride was wounded by her conceit.

'You have a pretty smart answer for everything.'

'Thank you for the compliment.'

Maybe she needed some deflating.

'But what about Evan Gregg?' Sam asked grimly. 'I'd say you weren't so smart there. How did he get to horn in on your game? Put you in a bit of a jam, hasn't it? Specially seeing as it was your man Hopkirk that cooked his goose.'

145

Lorraine scowled, spoiling her hand-some looks.

'I guess. But it was past time for him to collect what he was asking for! The spying rat interfered on his own account. He got wind of what I had going with Hopkirk and stole the newspaper cuttings. I'm sure he had the notion he could ingratiate himself by spilling the beans to either John Snyder or his daughter — whichever doesn't matter. The dumb galoot reckoned Sarah's fair hand and a share of the Diamond S would be his reward.'

Sam was astonished by the range queen's twisted thinking. It was inconsistent.

Gregg had pursued what he'd considered his own best interests and Lorraine painted that as disloyalty, which it might have been. Meanwhile, she was prepared to act covertly against members of her own family by marriage — and a man who'd actually shown her generosity in difficult times for whatever reason — to revive her fortunes with bounty money.

At best, she should have brought her suspicions and information to the proper legal authorities. The ruthlessness of her chosen course of action that would bring personal profit took Sam's breath.

It was like Lorraine had stripped her soul for him to see, black and corrupt. And she was so amoral, she couldn't see the ignominy in what she was admitting.

The poise and confidence she'd developed in bygone years before admiring audiences as a professional opera-house artiste had become distorted into a total love of self. Codes must be bent if they didn't suit her plans. She was a law unto herself. Wicked to the brink of insanity.

She'd told him a whole heap, but Sam remembered with a sudden leap of alarm that several of the most important questions he'd put to her still hadn't been answered.

'You said you knew where Dick Slick,

or John Snyder as you reckon, is hiding out.'

Lorraine shook her head. 'Didn't,' she said coolly. 'I said yes to knowing it was someplace around Rainbow. I think Sarah knows, and Hopkirk will make her tell.'

Sam felt a sinking feeling in his stomach.

'Do you know the methods a scoundrel of that stripe is likely to apply?'

'I hardly care, as long as he gets results.'

Sam saw that if he was going to save Sarah from an unpleasant fate he was going to have to use the few usable cards he had in his hand to maximum effect.

He'd have to call up histrionic abilities of his own.

'Lorraine,' he murmured, shaking his head sadly. 'I'm surprised at you. Once Hopkirk knows where Dick Slick is, the last thing he's going to do is deal someone else in on a slice of the reward money. He'll get the drop on his man and take him in on his own account, dead or alive. I know his kind. He'll want all the pie, not half. You won't see him again.'

Even to Sam's own ears, it sounded like it might be the truth.

Lorraine's jaw dropped. 'Do you really think so? Are you sure?'

'Sure I'm sure!' he said airily, as though it didn't matter.

'Why! That's — that's criminal!' Lorraine burst out. 'After I supplied him with all the leads he could possibly need.'

Sam managed to look shamefaced and shuffled his boots some.

'Damned if I haven't put my big ugly foot in it,' he said ruefully. 'Guess we all make mistakes . . . Mind you, it might be just my imagination running away with me.'

'But what if it isn't? Supposing he does intend to cheat me? How do we stop him?'

Sam noted the 'we' with satisfaction.

He'd got the fish hooked. She'd taken the bait, now he had to pull in the line.

He lowered his brows, pretending to think. Then, 'You suggested you had a hunch where Hopkirk might've taken Sarah,' he said in a casual tone. 'You tell me and maybe I'll ride there fast and check it out. See if Sarah's told the dirty son anything.'

Lorraine seized on the proposal with alacrity, the light of urgency in her eyes.

'Yes! Of course . . . I have to get back in on the deal. You're right, Sam. And I'll go there with you, so the bastard knows he isn't going to be allowed to welsh on me.'

Sam knew he'd lost any trace of feeling he might have had for Lorraine, yet he daren't let it show. The widow's greed and indifference to the fate of her young niece left him feeling sick. She was the last person whose company he wanted. But he also saw her as Sarah Snyder's slim chance of rescue. He depended on her co-operation to reveal the girl and Hopkirk's whereabouts.

He hoped too much vital time had not already been wasted.

'Ain't nothing holding us back, Lorraine,' he said with an eagerness that in a qualified way was genuine.

Lorraine laughed coarsely. 'We'll ride stirrup to stirrup. I've an idea I'm going to be a rich woman again real soon, Mr Hammond. Who knows? Maybe this is exactly what it'll take to trigger other rides . . . '

'Show me the way,' Sam drawled, and underlined the invitation with a sweep of his hat toward the door.

'My, are things getting that desperate, Sam?'

'Well, I don't know how long this excursion is going to take.'

Her eyes sparkled. 'It isn't more than an hour's fast ride from here. I told Hopkirk it would be a good place for quiet interrogations if such were necessary. Remember that old shack that was the Triple S's northern line-camp?'

Sam felt a glimmering of relief.

'Thought you were going to keep me

in suspense for ever. Let's go!' he rapped. 'I hate to figure Herb Hopkirk is getting away with any of this horseshit.'

She flung her arms around his neck in stagey passion, kissed him full on the lips and moustache and pressed her body hard against him.

'My favourite sheriff!'

Sam disentangled himself, trying not to show his revulsion.

'I said, let's go!'

★   ★   ★

Once out on the range, they spurred their horses to a fast lope. Eventually, Sam began to scan the earth for sign. Some reassurance that Lorraine had put him on the right track wouldn't go amiss.

As they rode on to rising ground and into scattered clumps of timber, he saw the confirmation he wanted without needing to dismount and check. Hitting a rough sidetrail, he pointed to the buggy's wheel tracks, hoofprints and at one point fresh horse droppings.

'Look! Reckon they came this way sure enough! Not more'n an hour previous.'

'What clever detective work!' Lorraine flattered him.

It wasn't true. Any good cowman could read such easy sign.

Sam lied through his teeth. 'It's a matter of training over a long spell, Lorraine.'

They heard the scream when the line shack was barely in sight between the oaks. It cut spine-chillingly through the dusk.

Sam was no longer troubled by just his imaginings. A girl who made a sound like that was in a hole — maybe a hole too deep for him to pull her out. The worry occurred to him, not for the first time, that once Hopkirk had the information he wanted from Sarah, it might well suit him to dispose of her. Dead men — or women — told no tales, and who was to deny that, say, a buggy spill could happen?

Her life was plumb in danger.

Sam urged his horse into one mad last dash and flung from the saddle while it was still moving.

The dim interior of the noisome shack was made considerably more horrific by the scene it staged. Sam saw a petrified girl he scarcely recognized, lashed half-naked to a bedstead, eyes glazed with fear, mouth open, able to utter only whimpers of terror. A sheen of sweat and a fiendish tracery of fierce red scratches were on her breasts.

Sam was familiar with the sight of Sarah Snyder around Rainbow City. Genuinely pretty with blue eyes, a straight nose, a wide mouth, a firm chin. Fashionably dressed in bonnet and dress, or maybe sombrero and riding-skirt. Proper. Lady-like.

He'd also seen her nude — completely, innocently at the swimming hole — but here, in her ripped-open upper clothing and spreadeagled, she looked something else. Worse almost than the cheapest whore at Jenny Abernethy's.

A snarling man, armed with a knife, was backing away from her at the interruption of the hoofbeats outside and his entry.

'You dirty bastard, Hopkirk!' Sam rasped, his heart like lead. 'You're under arrest!'

He went to draw his Colt, but Hopkirk lunged at him with the knife. The poor light, the hard ride, or maybe one of a hundred other unconsidered disadvantages, handicapped Sam.

He fumbled his draw, dropping the gun, and found himself fighting for his life with a younger, iron-muscled man. The knife drove for his throat.

He grabbed Hopkirk's knife-arm with his left hand and forced a sweeping slash aside. His clenched right fist went upwards and caught Hopkirk under the chin in a powerful jab.

Hopkirk dropped the knife.

It was not enough. In the half-light, Hopkirk seemed to fall back, but it was only a momentary retreat before he renewed his attack without the blade. His clenched teeth showed between lips peeled back in a brutish grin.

'You've got a licking coming to you, Mr Nosy Sheriff!'

Foot to foot, they exchanged meaty punches to both body and head.

Sam grunted.

Hopkirk groaned.

Sam delivered a flurry of blows under the range dick's ribs, his fists going like twin pistons. Hopkirk's head came down. Sour air surged out of his mouth with a retching sound.

Sam dodged nimbly to one side. There were no Marquis of Queensberry rules in this place at this time. He twisted his fingers into Hopkirk's hair. He yanked his head back and hit him again under his square jaw.

Hopkirk gagged and his grey face darkened, the scar standing out livid. But he didn't go down; wasn't out of the fight yet. He tottered and came up against the wall with a crash that shook the flimsy shack. Pushing off, he jack-knifed into a crouch, fists hanging loose at his sides, and circled Sam warily. Spittle pinkened by blood drooled out of the corner of his mouth.

They glared at each other, panting from the punishment yet seeming undaunted by their bruises and swellings, the bloody splits where skin over bone had been opened.

Hopkirk wasn't going to charge in again. He regained his breath, then cocked his fists, feinted and danced away as though daring Sam to leap into the attack.

'Arrest me, huh?' he taunted. 'I don't think so!'

Sam kept all his attention focused on the weaving man.

'You're going to get mussed up something fierce 'less you quieten down and give in peaceable!' he hurled back.

Sarah began screaming again with distracting, heart-rending urgency. Or was she trying to tell him something?

Suddenly, a savage, chopping blow

from behind exploded across the back of his neck.

Sarah spoke some words he could make sense of. *'Oh my God!'* But then all he could hear was a swelling, roaring noise like a deafening waterfall. His legs buckled. He dropped on to his knees. He tried to get up again, but his body wouldn't respond. He pitched forward into blackness.

11

Ugly Persuasion

Lorraine Delrose swung the rung she'd pulled from a broken straight-backed chair. It was a heavy, turned piece of oak. Her magnificence was regal only in the way of the cruel queen of a primitive jungle tribe. She gloated.

'Hit him in just the right spot, didn't I?' she said to Hopkirk. 'I take it since you're still here the little miss has failed to tell you what we want to know, despite your bully-boy tactics. Now I'll never know whether you planned to run out on me like Sam Hammond tried to kid me.'

Hopkirk mopped blood from a gashed brow and wriggled a loosened tooth with his tongue.

'Damned lawdog! 'Course I ain't running out on you. We got an agreement, and it stands. We get the gal to talk. It's the only way. Snyder'll be a dead man then. We'll pick up the bounty on his head — maybe some of his hidden stash, too. All those bank robberies, he has to have some left over.'

Lorraine smiled and her eyes glistened with a strange light.

'Let's not get ahead of ourselves, Mr Hopkirk. Sam Hammond thought he fooled me with his playacting, but I can see through men. I've been married to two of them and known a sight more than Sam's known women — the poor sucker.'

She kept swinging the dangerous rung like a baton.

'I've got your measure, too, Herb Hopkirk. I've left sealed papers at the bank to be opened in the event of my sudden death or disappearance. So I can't be cheated anyways.'

Hopkirk said sullenly, 'Think of everything, don't you?'

'I try to be smart. Well, smarter than most.'

She gestured at the knife on the dirt floor and at Hopkirk's pathetic prisoner, who was sobbing on the bed, straining against her bonds.

'Poor Miss Sarah! What a mess you've made of her prettiness!'

Then she went from scoffing to harsh seriousness.

'The knife was a mistake. More of those scratches and even washing off the blood won't make them look accidental or self-inflicted.'

She ran the thick, ridged chair rung up and down through a fisted left hand. It was hard and solid and smoothly tapered at the unbroken end, though it widened by several abrupt degrees to the substantial diameter of the rings of its mid-part, eight inches in.

Chillingly, she said, 'There's things I could do with this that won't leave obvious, external injuries. Mark my words, a hoity-toity miss like her who has never been in company with a man can soon be persuaded to talk.'

Hopkirk licked his swollen lips.

'Now why didn't I think of something like that?'

'Never mind that you didn't. Get Hammond trussed up first, and if the silly girl hasn't been provoked into divulging what we want to know, I'll hand over and let you give her reluctance the *coup de grâce*.'

⋆ ⋆ ⋆

Sam Hammond felt consciousness seeping back. From what seemed a long way off, the sounds of soft crying came to his ears. He thought he'd never heard anything sadder, more heartbroken.

Forcing his eyes open, he noted that the light in the shack had not deteriorated overmuch. He figured he'd been out of the world no more than a half-hour.

As well as the same poor light, his surroundings had the same stench of decay. But his nostrils flared, reacting to a subtle addition. The sweat of exertion? More blood?

Sam realized it was Sarah Snyder who was crying, still splayed on the bed where he'd last seen her. More of her clothing looked disarranged and the pitiful sight was more enraging to him than ever. Her quiet sobs pierced to his soul.

Herb Hopkirk was gone and he was alone with the girl.

'Hold on, Miss Sarah,' he said, his voice thick and awkward. 'I'll come and get you loose from there.'

As the words left his damaged lips, he realized how stupid they were. He was tied hand and foot himself and his aching head was still spinning.

'Oh!' Sarah said. 'I was afraid she'd killed you! She hit the back of your head so hard with the awful piece of chair.'

'Who . . . ?' Sam said. In his dazed state, he was only now starting to figure out what had happened to him and by whose hand.

Sarah gulped and sniffed. 'Lorraine Delrose, of course. She arrived with you, but attacked you while you were fighting with that beast Hopkirk.'

'Hell! They've hurt you, too, haven't they?'

'Yes,' she said in a small, trembling voice. 'I can't tell how bad. I'm sore and bruised and throb all over. The worst thing is, it hurt so bad I thought I'd die from the pain so I told them what they wanted to know. Now I wish I *had* died!'

She broke into a new bout of sobbing.

He could think of nothing to say to console her.

'Sh-Sheriff Hammond! I must have lost my mind. They got me to say where my daddy went to hide. He said there were people who were looking for him and he didn't want to see them. They mean to kill him, I know!'

'No, they won't!' Sam said forcefully, though his inner confidence fell far short of his tone. 'We'll get out of here and put a stop to their foul shenanigans!'

'How?' Sarah wailed.

Desperately, Sam looked around the primitive shack. And a pulse of elation went through him. He saw there was a good chance he could break out of his bonds.

The means would be the broken, upturned chair. The jagged, splintered stump of the removed rung's tenon protruded from the left front leg.

'Chin up! We're not sunk yet, kid. Just let me get myself untied and I'll have you freed, too.'

Sam rolled and shuffled on his backside till he was up against the solid old chair. He raised his wrists, and began to saw the rope against the jutting, hard splinters of oak.

The rope Hopkirk had found was half-rotten, like most everything else in the place. It parted faster than Sam had dared hope. His strong fingers made short work of the knots at his ankles.

What he saw when he went to cut Sarah loose, using his knife, appalled him. He worked anxiously, massaging the blood back into her hands and feet.

'I swear the bastards'll die for this alone. Will you be able to get up and move?'

'I th-think so,' Sarah stammered.

'Here,' Sam said, pulling off clothes. 'Have my shirt — I can go without it.'

She covered herself, leaving the bloodstained and knife-ripped tatters of her own upper garments where they fell, while Sam put back on his vest.

'Thank God they didn't kill you,' he said with what encouragement he could muster. 'You can tell me where they're headed. They made a bad mistake, leaving us alive.'

Sarah shivered and sniffed. 'They didn't think so. They had it all worked out.'

'How?'

'They reckon once they've — brought in my father, it'll be put about you were in cahoots with the Dick Slick gang, allowing Pa to hide out in your section in exchange for rich bribes.'

Sam's face hardened. 'I see. But how

about what they've done to you? How could they explain away the condition they've left you in?'

She said bitterly, 'I'll be painted as a — a lying slut! The tale will go I used my body to trade with Hopkirk for my father's safety. I bought him off, making advances, tempting him with charms and wiles. Tried to seduce him from his honest, law-abiding purpose . . . '

'That's vile!'

'They are vile people,' she said, her voice gaining the strength of indignation about what she'd suffered at their hands. 'I've always hated my aunt!'

Sam had enough sentimentality about him to regret that hatred could be embedded in one so young, but he couldn't fault her for it. Not now. Lorraine Delrose had stolen Sarah's innocence and freshness. The hatred was as justified as it was deeply felt.

His own feeling in the matter was powerful.

'I'm going to avenge this, Sarah. No

father can have sinned more than you've been sinned against here. Tell me quickly, where are your aunt and Hopkirk headed? Where is your pa?'

Sarah hesitated in customary reflex to the dread question put to her so often of late. Then, giving in, as she'd already done to Lorraine Delrose and Herb Hopkirk, she croaked, 'The abandoned mine . . . the old Horsehead Mine.'

★   ★   ★

In Sam's mind, Horsehead Mine existed as a piece of history. A group of Californians had set up operations north of Rainbow City in the 1860s, placing reliance on Germans for expertise in metallurgy and chemistry and on Cornishmen for excavation. They'd established extensive underground workings, a stamp mill and a large plant for treating crushed ore.

But problems with flooding and pumping saw the ambitious Californians' capital reserves dwindle rapidly. The veins began petering out. Shafts filled to mining levels with ice-cold water. The pumps clogged with gritty sludge. Returns fell and fell.

Within ten years, the Californians had quit, redirecting investment to real estate and land development at the scenes of former successes.

Now, Horsehead was a place of junk piles and dumps, dangerous holes in the ground, and the ruins of a once-rowdy and lawless camp. The miners and those who'd preyed on them had departed, while the squalor and desolation of the site had yet to attract any romance. It was just unlovely history . . .

Sam reflected that all of life was history in the making in point of fact, his own life included and pretty damn poor making that was. No home of his own, no woman, no sons, no daughters. He had nothing to show for his efforts, except maybe a town he'd thought he'd tamed and was tolerably peaceable . . . till the likes of a Herb Hopkirk rode the stage in and proved how impermanent the peace could be.

Sarah Snyder — pretty, proper daughter of a leading family — could be raped. Her father could be unmasked as a fugitive bank robber. Her aunt could show her true colours as a grasping, cold-hearted hussy, sinking to obscene crimes in the pursuit of money, furthering them as an accomplice without mercy or feeling.

Everything changed shockingly — more and more, often overnight, it seemed — as he grew older. When change was about the only thing a man thought he could count on, wasn't that a sign he was growing old?

What was he living for? What was he working for?

★　★　★

Sam said heavily, 'Then that's what I have to do — I have to ride to the Horsehead Mine pronto. Could be something can be saved yet from this godawful mess.'

On a hunch, he picked up a dilapidated bull's-eye lantern he'd noted lying among the litter about the shack. He shook it. The slosh of lamp-oil was reassuring. It was about half-full.

'I'll need light, prowling around those old workings,' he allowed. 'I'll get back soon as I can.'

Sarah's eyes flew wide. 'Oh, no! You mustn't leave me here alone! I'll come with you.'

'But it could be risky.'

'No more risky than staying here. Supposing they — you don't find them, and they come back? They'd probably kill me for sending you after them.'

Sam nodded, understanding what she was saying, her fear. She was suffering from shock, too, he realized. She sat stiffly on the edge of the bed, staring at nothing except, maybe, something burned on her mind's eye. She breathed in heaves, the air making small catching sounds in her throat.

'I don't like it,' he said, 'but I guess it'll be better that way.'

To say whatever lay in store at Horsehead Mine might do her harm would be stupid, considering how much she'd already suffered. Briefly, he wondered if, despite her fear of a violent death, she might be wanting to die. Violated young women in this day and age were known to take their lives. But Sam trusted to his instincts. Sarah Snyder didn't seem the suicidal sort.

'Are you — are your arms and legs in working order yet?' he asked.

She nodded. 'I think so.'

'Then let's go.'

Another frustration awaited outside. Sam's horse had gone.

'Hopkirk is a hoss thief to boot!' Sam grumbled.

Sarah reminded, 'But we have the buggy. The Horsehead road is still passable for wheeled vehicles most of its length. We can still make it there. Maybe we'll be in time . . . '

To a low moon and the stars dimly making their presence shown in the evening sky, Sam made a vow that they would.

12

Family Secrets

Sam Hammond fed the pair of matching blacks the whip frugally, which was enough to set the fine animals into a brisk, mile-eating pace. They were a pair of matched pacers Sarah's father had brought all the way from Kentucky. Without question, they would have cost him plenty. The girl was justifiably proud of them, though Sam knew she was in no state right now to appreciate any of her life's pleasures.

Before long the road began a gradual, winding ascent into foothills. Sarah shivered.

'Better put the blanket over your knees,' Sam said. 'It's getting colder.'

In fact, he scarcely felt it himself though great black clouds were rolling up from the east and there was a hint of rain in the air. She was probably in shock.

'I hate her!' she burst out suddenly. 'It was a fair and square fight before she hit you from behind. You would've beaten Hopkirk and none of the rest would have happened. She's evil!'

Sam didn't want to dwell on it — nor want Sarah to — but he said almost involuntarily, 'The worst was what they did to you. I can't believe it.'

Unexpectedly, Sarah said more as she tucked the blanket round her legs and shrank back into the cushions.

'You would if you knew the complete, secret history of the Snyder family.'

'Oh . . . ?'

'With my aunt it has always been her first and all the time. What she wants she goes after and fights to get, no matter the cost to others, even kin.'

Sam wondered where these bitter thoughts, and the intriguing suggestion of secrecy, were leading.

'I know that . . . And that the

Snyders were part of the Rainbow City landscape long before I came along. Lorraine was already your uncle's wife, too, which made her a Snyder in most folks' eyes, though it was only by marriage.'

Sarah blinked her eyes quickly as though to fight back tears. In the glance Sam shot her, he couldn't tell if they were caused by emotion, or just the wind they were whipping in their rush through the coming dark.

She said, 'Much of what's significant happened before my time as well — before I was born. Folks outside the closest family have never been told.'

But Sarah wanted to tell him. Sam could sense it, despite the smallness of her choked voice, despite the urgency of their journey. He wanted to say, 'Go on'; decided that might be a mistake. She had to take her time although they might have so little.

They'd reached the first stiff grade and the blacks had slowed to a walk. Sam drew rein at the crest of the rise, pulling them to complete rest. He gestured at the deepening twilight. 'I have to light the lamps,' he explained.

The glow seemed to promote friendly intimacy under the dark, boiling sky. Sarah licked her lips.

'It happened in San Francisco when Lorraine Delrose first met my father, John Snyder. My father has always been a free-spending man, with a penchant for the high life. It wouldn't have been hard for her to learn that he was the son of a rich cattleman.'

Sarah's voice dropped to a broken whisper. 'Anyway, she married him secretly after a whirlwind romance.'

Sam was incredulous. 'Your father? *John* Snyder?'

'Yes, John Snyder . . . but he wasn't my father then, of course — just a rather silly young bachelor in the Paris on the Pacific with a taste for good things, which included glamorous opera singers. Then his brother turned up in 'Frisco . . . '

'Rex Snyder. His older brother.'

'Exactly. La Delrose knew John was in line to inherit much of his father's rich cattle ranch. It was part of his attraction for her, I'm sure. But Rex, being the elder, would be due to inherit the best, the richest acres. Potentially, he therefore represented an even better catch. My daddy was furious when he found his brother in bed with his wife.'

'Lordy . . . ' Sam breathed. 'What ructions that would've caused!'

Sarah licked her lips again. 'No, not really. Sanity prevailed. A quick divorce and remarriage was agreed upon — also that the sordid matter should be kept from the two brothers' dying father at home on the Big S. Despite what the woman and Rex had done, the family name had to be kept clear and honourable in the Rainbow country! Part of the settlement between the two brothers was that Rex should cede the best part of his inheritance, the land by the river, to John by way of compensation.'

The lamplight strong on his face,

Sam tried not to let his astonishment show.

'You mean John swopped Lorraine for some land? Didn't that make things kind of difficult when they went on living in the same section?'

'I don't think so. My father wasn't the man for Lorraine at all. She probably married him only for his money. And maybe the land actually eased hard feelings over the infidelity. Leastways, between the brothers . . . I don't think Lorraine ever came to terms with its forfeiture. She always meant Uncle Rex, or herself, to have it back somehow.'

'But what Lorraine told me indicated your pa wanted to get back together with her again after she was widowed, reuniting the two spreads. That it was she who was unwilling.'

Sarah sighed jerkily.

'All I'm sure of is that after Lorraine was unfaithful to him, Daddy met my mother and she was consolation enough for him through the many years until she died. I think he then found it very hard to live without a woman at his side. A change came over him. Not that he was any less considerate to me or his ranch foreman and crew, but he was moody. Withdrawn. The frequent trips away began. To start with, I thought he was just escaping the general atmosphere of grief and misery, especially when hard times came locally to the cattle business. Who could blame Papa for wanting to go someplace where he could kick up his heels?'

Sam avoided bringing up the possibly alienating subject of Dick Slick. He had yet to figure where his duties and his loyalties lay. Were the two conflicted?

'Lorraine told me your pa gave her money to see the Triple S over the difficulties.'

'Oh, Papa was such a fool!' Sarah said in sudden despair. 'He thought that Lorraine, being alone like himself, would marry him again, if only he brought her all the wealth she could desire!'

Sam urged the team back into a fast trot. He had much to think about. For the next twenty minutes neither he nor Sarah tried to speak in competition with the steady drum of hoofs, the whirr of the spinning wheels and the jolts and rattles of the buggy as the road surface became increasingly uneven.

The swift blacks brought them to a place where the trail plunged into a ravine, crossed a bridge and climbed back to the higher ground.

As they headed down the incline the horses were barely able to keep the buggy from over-running them. Sam used the brake, though not too viciously that the wheels would lock and put them into an uncontrollable slide.

'The road might be passable, but it's getting mighty dangerous on these steep bits,' he said. 'Horsehead Mine won't be any safer, specially if Hopkirk and your pa get to exchanging shots.'

Clinging to the seat with white-knuckled hands and ready to jump the instant they might tip, Sarah dared to take her eyes off the road and said tensely, 'You're not going to back out, are you?'

Sam said with grim humour, 'The county'll take care of the cost of my burying, but I don't know about yourself.'

The rig rattled across the planking of a bridge at the bottom of the ravine. Beneath them rushed the roaring headwaters of Rainbow Creek that eventually weaved placidly through the bottomlands on the Diamond S. Sam had to use the whip to encourage the faltering blacks up the far slope.

Hardy brush crowded closely on either side and big rocks littered the sloping trail.

When conversation became possible again, Sam went on, 'I plan to leave you hidden with the buggy in that clump of trees up yonder. Are your blacks broken to the saddle?'

'Yes, but what do you mean, leave me?'

'Just that. It'll be safest for you.'

She collapsed against him, despair on her face. Sam caught a glimpse, too, of dread — a touch of horror.

She said chokily, 'I want to go to my father.'

The twisted piñon trees, and amongst them the dark grey rocks splashed with scabrous lichen, didn't look inviting shelter. The gathering clouds above portended a wet night.

'He may not want to be found,' Sam said.

Plainly, John Snyder was in huge trouble. His daughter's presence would be of little comfort to a man in his situation, on the dodge from the law. Lady Luck had deserted Dick Slick at last. Snyder was an intelligent man who must have realized the jig was up, unless his reasoning faculties had also deserted him. In the best interests of the world in which the unoffending, like his Sarah, had to make their way, the laws of the land had to be enforced. Bank robbers who killed in the execution of their crimes must pay the penalty or seek pardon, of which there was dim chance.

Sam doubted he could salvage much from the mess Snyder had descended into, but the avarice and barbarism of his present evil hunters threatened him with a fate that had less to recommend it than the scaffold. Justice would be ill-served by a ruthless bounty hunter and a scheming Jezebel. The methods they'd employed with Sarah, an innocent party, were inexcusable.

The pair were living proof of the axiom that there was no God west of the Missouri. The almighty dollar was their divinity and they were, to Sam's mind, worshippers more single-minded than Sarah's misguided parent.

Sam added with greater confidence than he felt, 'Hopkirk and Lorraine Delrose went off half-cocked. I don't reckon they'll find your pa either. The old mine workings are a subterranean maze. Roaming around them in the dark is asking for trouble in any case, but I'm willing to give it a try. Alone.'

At his adamant tone, Sarah lapsed into white-faced silence.

Under the low canopy of the trees, Sam stripped the harness from one of the blacks, but left its bridle on. He doused the buggy's lamps, attached the unlit bull's-eye lantern they'd brought from the line shack to his belt, and pulled himself up on to the back of the horse.

'What exactly do you intend to do?' Sarah asked.

'Hopkirk and Lorraine weren't that far ahead of us. First off, I figure on surprising and arresting the pair of them at gunpoint. They've crimes of their own that must be answered for. It'll be a surer thing than finding your father.'

And a fairer, Sam thought, which spurred guilt in him. Maybe he was getting too old and sentimental to function as an effective peace officer.

The black was unhappy about being mounted bareback, but being worn out, it only tossed its head and snorted. Sam clapped his heels to its sweaty sides and was off at a lope before Sarah could frame more questions or objections.

Although she called after him from the screening copse, he couldn't make out the words and didn't answer.

A fine, chill rain began to fall.

Sam didn't really mind that, then. Well, hell — most of the country could do with a spell of rain, couldn't it?

13

We'll Flush Him Out!

Horsehead Mine was a truly dismal place in the last, failing light of day. Lorraine Delrose had taken in the evidence of its closed operations along the deteriorating road. It was some years since she'd ridden this way and the signs were all of destruction and devastation.

At one time, the stamping and crushing mills and a smelting works had filled the vicinity with hubbub and smoke by night and day. Now, the place appeared deserted. The digging, burrowing, gulching and sluicing had left an unlovely landscape. Not even regenerating tangles of brush could hide the scars. The hillsides were littered with the charred stumps of nature's despoiled, former greenery.

An owl hooted mournfully from the high safety of a skeletal structure that had once housed a hoist over one of many shafts giving access to what Lorraine knew was an underground labyrinth of excavations. Maybe with the sky threatening rain, it was not going to be a good night for the owl's hunting of rats and the other small vermin that infested the ruins and were its prey.

Too bad for the owl, Lorraine thought. She was buoyed by the knowledge a $3,000 bounty was afoot someplace here. Also in the offing was the Dick Slick bank robbery stash that could amount to much, much more. John Snyder was going to learn that crime didn't pay — leastways not the poor fools who perpetrated it. Her and Hopkirk's hunting, unlike the hooting owl's, could scarcely fail to go unrewarded . . . could it?

Herb Hopkirk drew rein beside her.

'What a dump! Where the hell do we look for the bastard?'

A first drift of rain augmented the beads of sweat on his corpse-white face and trickled down the darker line of the old scar.

Lorraine cast her straining eyes over the huddle of the mine's ramshackle buildings. Breathless, gathering darkness hung over the scene. The abandoned settlement looked like one big graveyard to futile endeavour. Weed-strewn, potholed roadways led between rotting, tumbledown buildings mostly of log and clapboard.

She felt frustration. 'I don't rightly know. Snyder's girl might've given us more details. Could be we should've brought her along.'

'Well, we didn't,' Hopkirk said impatiently. 'We'll have to search closer and fast while there's still light left. I suggest we dismount, circle the place separately and meet back here to confer. You go left, I'll go right.'

It sounded appropriate and satisfying to Lorraine.

'Good. There aren't that many places

sound enough for shelter and hiding. Once we know where he is, we'll flush him out!'

★ ★ ★

Dusk was deepening into night and the patter of rain was settling the Horse-head Mine dust. Before he'd slipped from his horse and tethered it to a warped but solid hitch-rail, Herb Hopkirk had made his own appraisal of the mine buildings and decided where he'd be looking first.

The cabin was on a ridge, slightly apart from neighbouring erections and showed signs of repair. Boards had been nailed over broken siding, the windows had shutters and a piece of tin formed a still shiny patch on the sagging roof.

When he drew closer, the clincher caught Hopkirk's attention immediately.

It was an open padlock which hung in the staple of the unclosed hasp. The lock, with the key in it, was too new to

190

have rusted. That it wasn't in use suggested the owner was present, inside the cabin.

Hopkirk gave a quick glance around. Lorraine Delrose was out of sight and he figured her involvement would be more hindrance than help.

Holding the drawn Smith & Wesson lightly in his right fist at waist level, Hopkirk padded swiftly upslope to the cabin. Rain-dampened dust attached itself and clung grittily to his boots.

'Sure as hell, somebody must be here,' he murmured.

He slid along the cabin wall to the closed door. Nothing happened. Nobody challenged him; likely, nobody had seen him.

He reached out and warily turned the door knob. Then, in a rush, he raised his left foot and booted the door fully open.

It swung on well-oiled hinge pins to smash back against the inner wall with a loud, splintering crash. Hopkirk followed it through and flattened himself against its planking, gun raised and cocked.

The cabin was empty.

But Hopkirk had made no mistake about the place being in present use. Blankets were on a bunk. A tin plate and a mug were on a three-legged table propped up with broken lumber. A lantern hung from a low roof beam. Packing-case cupboards held a few cans of food and cardboard boxes of candles and matches; two bottles of whiskey.

No bank money. No proof that 'Dick Slick' had been here.

Was it Snyder's hideout, or just some innocent vagabond's temporary retreat?

Hopkirk scowled. Goddamn it, he could have sworn he'd struck his own kind of gold at this here Horsehead Mine. He was turning away in sour exasperation when he spotted the trapdoor in the wooden floor. It was half-covered by a piece of soiled, vermin-chewed carpet.

Maybe there was a cellar. Maybe the occupant had fled to it on his approach and the carpet had failed to flop back completely into position over the closing trapdoor . . .

Hopkirk hefted his revolver again, slammed the door to give the impression he was leaving . . . and catfooted across the floor to the trapdoor.

★ ★ ★

What Sarah Snyder cried out as Sam left her by the buggy under the trees was, 'I'll be damned if I'll stay here, Sheriff Hammond!'

Whatever her father had done, he was her pa. Hopkirk and her treacherous aunt were totally foul. Their interest in finding John Snyder had nothing to do with justice. They'd made no secret of it. What they were after was money. They were mercenaries of the darkest stripe.

Sarah, who'd never been left to want for much of anything she'd desired, found it hard to understand. Hopkirk and Lorraine Delrose had set aside principles and surely more appealing endeavours to do without scruples whatever it took to achieve success as measured in dollar terms. This encompassed her father's death.

Although Hopkirk called himself a detective, his pursuit of justice was different from Sheriff Hammond or Clint Freeman's. The dedication of both officers to upholding the law she could recognize somehow as a lifelong calling. They were unlikely to make big money from it, nor would they drop the cause if it ever did.

They would always fight cleanly and give a man a square deal.

Sarah readied the second black horse as she'd seen Sam do the first and mounted up. Straining her eyes into the growing darkness, she set off in pursuit.

The rain and the coming night put coldness into her. Icy fingers seemed to clutch at her very heart, making it beat faster.

Soon she could no longer pick out Sam's tracks through the slanting rain, but the trail to Horsehead Mine was clear enough, though broken and uneven because it had been left to fall into disrepair since the mine's closure. By the time the ruins of the mine buildings came into sight, she was breathing hard and her heart was pounding.

The dark buildings were sagging and paintless and conveyed an impression of decay and emptiness. Of desolation. She felt afraid.

She comforted herself with the thought that she must catch up with Sam now. While she was casting around for recent hoofprints, her horse abruptly gave a whinny that was answered from the shadows of a nearby thicket.

Sarah rode over, confident her black had found its partner and Sam for her.

She came across the horse by itself, tied to a bush and tearing hungrily at the tussocks of coarse grass thereabout. Sarah's hands clenched into fists so that her nails cut into the softness of her palms.

Where was Sam? Where should she look for him now?

Suddenly, with a swiftness that stopped her breath, she heard stealthy footsteps from behind. Before she could turn, an arm wrapped itself around her throat and something hard dug into her ribs.

★　★　★

Sam Hammond heard the crash of the cabin door above the incessant hiss of the rain. Flinging caution aside, he ran between the tumbledown, crumbling shacks, his feet picking up dust that had turned to cloying mud and would soon be under puddles.

He whipped the cold, blue steel of his Colt revolver from the holster at his hip. A feeling of unease churned his stomach. A foreboding of misfortune. He had a premonition Hopkirk and Lorraine had discovered John Snyder's hiding-place and murder was about to be done.

Hopkirk heaved up the trapdoor, revealing an oblong of wan light. Gun raised to shoulder level where it would be clearly visible, he peered in.

The first thing he noted was a startled face lit by a lantern placed on a table and turned low.

'Well, well, well,' Hopkirk said. 'Mr John Snyder, I presume. Alias Dick Slick!'

Horrified by the intrusion, the man in the cellar jumped up from the chair in which he sat, dropping a newspaper he'd been reading and reaching toward a gunbelt at the end of a bed.

He was lean and gaunt and of uncertain age. The shadows of his hidey-hole made him look more like an old scarecrow than an ostensibly successful cattleman with a taste for the high life.

'I wouldn't if I were you!' Hopkirk snapped. 'Touch that gun and from this close I'd blow your hand to bits sure.'

The cellar looked to be longer-term living quarters than the cabin above. Hopkirk determined the hole in the ground was Snyder's real bolt-hole.

As his eyes grew accustomed to the weak light, he noted a section of panelling at one side adorned with shirts and changes of clothing, some of them quite fancy, hanging from wooden pegs. Elsewhere were shelves holding a wash bowl and pitcher, shaving mug, brush and straight razor. A large, brown-spotted mirror was tacked on a tilt between two horizontal wooden beams bracing an uneven earthen wall.

Along from the bed were piles of staple supplies: sacks of flour and beans, a cask of sugar, a side of smoke-cured bacon, more canned goods and a small barrel of crackers.

A burlap curtain covered the wall at the far end of the cellar.

'Nearly all the comforts of home,' Hopkirk sneered, looking down.

The disturbed man thought better of his rash move toward his gun and drew back behind the table.

'Yeah, I'm John Snyder, but what's this with the Dick Slick business?'

'Don't play the innocent with me, Snyder. It won't wash. I'm a detective and it's my job to uncover the secret lives of criminals. All I need to know from you is where you've hidden your loot.'

Snyder shrugged thin shoulders.

'All right, I'm a bank robber and have been caught,' he said stoically. 'That's all I have to say. Kill me if you must, then no one will ever find the cache. Or hear the confession I was Dick Slick.'

Hopkirk calculated rapidly. Were the bank robbery proceeds more than the bounty money? Could he let Snyder bargain for his life with the loot? Could he collect *both*?

He was mulling over the dilemma when in Snyder's brown-spotted mirror he caught a suggestion of movement behind him.

He whirled, triggering, and all hell broke loose.

14

The Finishing Shot

In response to the ingrained caution developed in the latter years of his sheriffing, Sam Hammond slackened his run as he approached the cabin with the open door.

He detected a glimmer of light from within.

He left the track, flattened himself against alley walls and slid along them toward the doorway.

He reached a gurgling rain barrel but crouched behind it no more than a second. For now he could hear voices, one of which was Hopkirk's.

He hefted his gun and set his mouth grimly. Cold water trickled down his neck and past his collar. He eased forward slowly. He inched to the door and whatever was in progress inside the shuttered cabin.

Clearer words reached his ears above the patter of the falling rain.

'... *That's all I have to say. Kill me if you must, then no one will ever find the cache. Or hear the confession I was Dick Slick.*'

He knew that voice. John Snyder!

It was time, Sam thought, to take a hand.

But the instant he plunged through the door, Colt at the ready, a bullet whizzed over his head, parting his hair, and he was deafened by the thunder of gunfire.

In reflex, he returned the fire across what seemed momentarily to be an empty room and dropped to the floor. He rolled into cover behind a three-legged table, which he knocked off supporting lumber and tipped. Tinware clattered and careered across the floor. The tabletop then stood upright, like a barricade between himself and his opponent, who he figured from the direction in which he'd seen the muzzle flash was kneeling behind an open trapdoor in the floor.

Double damn, that had been mighty close! Almost as though the man — surely gun-swift Herb Hopkirk — had known he was there. How?

Sam felt more uncomfortable about this than anything else in his entire life — and he'd been in some pretty tight corners in his time. His insides felt like they'd gone to jelly, but it wasn't that he was consciously afraid. Uncertain, maybe. Depressed? Sure — about the thought that he wasn't going to see this episode through to a satisfactory conclusion; that others, like Sarah Snyder, might find themselves again at the mercy of Lorraine and Hopkirk.

Hopkirk was of professional gun-fighter breed. Blood-spilling came to him by habit. He reacted on instincts so acute they seemed inexplicable, unnatural. He killed at the merest provocation. And Sam had carried a fight to him.

Sam was getting too old for such a bold play! Again, he was faced with a gunfight too many.

Hopkirk cussed foully and yelled to him.

'Should've put out your lamps back there when I could, Sheriff Hammond, but it ain't too late yet. You got a gun and a chance. Stand up like a man and use 'em while you got the chance!'

Frantically, Sam racked his brains for some way to throw Hopkirk off his guard, to gain some instant's advantage whereby he could save his life.

He thought of nothing.

'The hell I will,' he bluffed. 'You're done for, Hopkirk! Cornered. Your killing and assaulting days are over. I'm waiting to take you in — you and Miss Delrose both.'

Hopkirk laughed and it was more a bark of disgust.

'Thought as much,' he jeered. 'You ain't got the sand to accommodate me, Hammond. You can walk tall and talk big in your Rainbow City, old man, but out here you're jumpy as a scared jack-rabbit. Sure you don't want to run?'

203

'You're the worst of frontier scum, Hopkirk! I'm arresting you. Throw down your gun and step out!'

It was like Sam had prodded a rattler. Hopkirk acted, and Sam winced even as he squeezed his own trigger. In a blur of action that was unreal in its eye-cheating speed, Hopkirk darted up from behind the trapdoor and fired. The roar of both their pistols merged into one great, eardrum-numbing blast.

Sam felt Hopkirk's shot slice burningly across his right ribs, but his own shot went wild, flying into the roof. He needed to fire again quickly, but the room rocked and seemed to sway. All strength fled from the muscles in his out-thrust gunarm. To his horror, he saw his weapon fall from any mark he might choose. It was as though he'd ceded control to the weighty iron to point as it would, even to the floor.

The acrid reek of gunsmoke filled the small cabin. Sam knew it was all over for him. Hopkirk would fire his third, killing shot at his cruel leisure, before the paralysing, breath-robbing pain in Sam's right side abated. Nothing would stop him. Sam had gotten himself into his last gunfight.

Hopkirk stood up behind the trapdoor, solid as a rock, his legs braced slightly apart, and raised the smoking Smith & Wesson. He took slow and careful aim at his incapacitated, helpless victim.

Time stood still in Sam's mind. His life didn't flash before his eyes. He felt no fear, no resignation, only enormous exasperation. He wondered if it was how a condemned man would feel in his last moments on the gallows when the black hood was over his head and the rope around his neck.

The reprieve was delivered with a new, ear-splitting crack and flash from the cellar beneath their feet.

They'd both forgotten John Snyder. The man who was the hunted Dick Slick was not averse to shooting his way out when his tail was in a crack. And the chance offering, he did it now.

Snyder's bullet took Hopkirk squarely in the back. He jerked up on his toes, his shattered spine arching as the misshapen lead exited in a gout of blood from his chest.

The gun tumbled with a clatter from his lifeless fingers. His bulky body seemed to collapse in comic slow motion. On his scarred white face was a blank stare of stupid surprise. His heavy body hit the floorboards with a crash that shook the building.

Sam watched in disbelief as the head of the man he'd known as a law-abiding rancher, young Sarah's father and a man with a professed taste for the civilized, cultural life, emerged from the opening in the floor to the cellar.

'You've killed him,' he said absurdly.

'Surely. There was no other option,' Snyder said more coolly than Sam could believe. 'He would've killed me after he'd killed you and helped himself to my hidden reserve of bank money. Didn't you know the straight of it, Hammond? Hopkirk had been tipped off by someone. I've been on the dodge from him for weeks. He pursued me relentlessly to Rainbow City, and he run me to earth here, God knows how.'

Sam shook his head regretfully. 'I've been told one hell of a lot about your business, Snyder. You're sick. Your robbing sprees prove it. And now I've got to take you in.'

Snyder flourished a long-barrelled Peacemaker at him. He grinned wryly, maybe with a mite of sympathy.

'I reckon not, Mr Sheriff. You look all washed up to me, howsoever well informed you opine yourself. My money was hard-gotten from the safes and vaults of the kind of institutions that would've carelessly seen me and others ruined by happenstance. I'm riding out of here with what's left of the cash haul. You'll never see me again.'

'What about your daughter?' Sam said in desperate appeal. He glanced briefly at Hopkirk's bleeding corpse. 'She's a fine girl. She was attacked by this piece of — carrion. You're her father. She needs you!'

'She wouldn't want to have a father who was sent to the scaffold.'

Sam felt his frustration rising. The situation had spun out of his control. Maybe he'd made a bad mistake in coming here alone. Hopkirk and Lorraine had seemed to present the real threat to the peace and security of the innocent; to be the most deserving of a lawman's urgent attention. But now Snyder had seized the upper hand and Sam was in no position to stop him walking out with a swag of bank money.

Sam clutched at his bruised and blood-sticky side. He lurched to his feet, knowing any fight he could offer was too feeble to be worth a damn.

He tasted gall. Gunplay would be suicidal. Snyder had his weapon cocked, ready to anticipate any move he made to use his own Colt.

Snyder moved into the cabin, away from the cellar's gaping aperture, covering him unwaveringly.

'Drop your gun and kick it over to

me,' he ordered.

But it was turn and turn about. Before Sam could comply, new elements were introduced that didn't so much reverse the situation as turn it on its head.

He froze as the sounds of struggle and heavy breathing came from the door behind him.

'Make one false move, either of you,' a voice shrilled, 'and I'll blow her head off her shoulders!'

15

Justice and Healing

Sam turned, doing nothing that could be construed as provocative. Then, beyond his ability to stop it, only a pulse beat in his throat.

Lorraine Delrose and Sarah Snyder were at the opening of the cabin door. The older woman held the frightened girl in front of her like a shield. The muzzle of a revolver was pressed to the girl's temple.

Lorraine shoved her captive into the room. Hair and clothes clung wetly to their heads and bodies. A first flash of lightning threw spectral white light across them.

Snyder recovered first. 'Well, who do we have here? Orphans of the storm,' he quipped.

'Shut up!' Lorraine snapped. 'Drop

your hardware, and lift your hands high — unless you want to see your filly's head blown apart! You, too, Sam Hammond!'

Sam and Snyder did as they were asked, Snyder shrugging.

'You must have lost your mind, Lorraine.'

'No! It's you who did that. They should have locked you up in the lunatic asylum.'

A long, rumbling roll of thunder swallowed her words and rocked the mining settlement. Rain swept down outside in sheets.

'So what next?' Snyder asked, seemingly unperturbed by her contemptuous estimation of his sanity.

'You're going to pay back for all the rocks you've strewn in the path of my ambitions — all the disappointments, the pains, the insult of your patronizing charity! Kick your guns to me across the floor . . . both of you!'

Snyder and Sam's guns slid to her feet.

'That's gratitude for you,' Snyder said in a tone of mild censure. 'I accept that as a young man my choice of bedmate was unfortunate, but I saved the Triple S from foreclosure.'

Sam said despairingly, 'Lorraine, I've had a gutful of your cunning and the murderous methods of your hired gunman, who's now dead — '

'Tcah! Hopkirk should have finished you back at the line shack, you loser! You'd seen enough to put him in the pen for life.'

She dipped and swiftly scooped up the surrendered revolvers, one at a time, thrusting them into her waistband. Her own gun she kept trained on Sarah throughout.

Sam ignored her scorn and went on. And this time his impressive moustache seemed to bristle as he spat words out of the side of his mouth, condemning her conduct.

'Your greed knows no bounds, Lorraine Delrose. You've no conscience, no scruples. Get your bank gold

— present your evidence against your brother-in-law and ex-husband, if that's what you prefer. But let Miss Sarah go free. You have my word I'll let you climb out of the pit you've dug for yourself. Maybe you can still save your soul from eternal ruin.'

She looked at him chillingly and he knew talk was no good. None of his words had reached her.

'You got it backward, Sheriff. I'm the one who's telling what's going to happen, and Miss Snyder's the one who'll have to look to the disposition of her soul if you interfere. She stays at gunpoint, close to me, standing surety for your good behaviour. I'm sticking up the stick-up man. If he keeps his head and hands over the money, his daughter will keep hers.'

Snyder said, 'You always were a heartless, avaricious bitch, Lorraine.'

Sarah blurted, 'She's crazy, Pa! Let her have the money.'

'I can't refuse her, can I? My sins have found me out and confounded me. I'm sorry, Sarah.'

Snyder backed to the cellar opening. Sam sensed he was putting on a brave face for the sake of Sarah, who looked petrified, but he suspected other thoughts and feelings lay beneath his bravado.

'It's in a knapsack stashed in a mine shaft, walled up at the end of a gouged-out vein,' Snyder said matter-of-factly. 'There's an entrance to the shaft from a tunnel that terminates in the cellar. You'll have to give me a minute or two to go down with a pick — '

'You go any place, I come with you,' Lorraine interrupted, eyes gleaming. 'So does the precious Sarah. There'll be no tricks played. Try to get away through that maze of tunnels down there, and she's dead. You, too, probably.'

Sam couldn't fault her clear thinking, mad though she might be. It was common knowledge locally the Californian mine promoters had created a labyrinth of excavations beneath the earth's rocky crust. The company had begun by sinking shafts into the main vein, first at 100, then 200, and finally 300 feet. As the depth increased, the company ran horizontal shafts intersecting the many vertical drops.

Sam had seen plans of the workings but he'd never been able to make head or tail of them. Anyhow, not sufficiently to put trust in them, considering many of the tunnels and shafts were now flooded and the shoring timbers ageing. Snyder evidently had better familiarized himself with the layout, and learned what parts of the jumble were safe. Few others had cared or dared to explore the mines since the closure. It would have been a good choice for an outlaw to locate his hidey-hole, provided he understood where the risks lay.

Snyder again gave no argument to his sister-in-law and one-time wife. 'Who goes down the cellar steps first?'

'You, then your daughter. Pull any stunts in the cellar and it'll be like

shooting fish in a barrel for me.'
Lorraine fixed Sam with a steely glare.
'And if you're gone when I return with
the money, Sheriff Hammond, the girl's
blood gets spilled anyway!'

So even if he hadn't been wounded
and disarmed, Sam knew no choice was
open to him at all but to wait and fume.

★   ★   ★

Sarah followed her father down the
steep steps into the cellar. Her loath-
some and contemptible aunt was close
on her heels. The end of a gun barrel
jabbed at her back, her neck, her head.
And it broke its terrifying contact for
only the briefest of moments in their
descent.

Her quivering lips moved sound-
lessly.

*Dear Lord, hear my pleas. I don't
want to die. Don't let the bitch kill me!*

She tried to think of something far
away, pleasant and homely to stave off
her growing sense of overwhelming

216

panic. The only picture she could call to mind was of Sam Hammond's tongue-tied deputy, the possibly now-crippled Clint Freeman, and he played no real part in her life and would never be of help to a girl, would he?

Her father went to the burlap curtain at the end of the cellar and thrust it aside. He gestured at the dark opening revealed.

'We'll need the lantern,' he said. 'Have I your permission?'

Lorraine laughed almost hysterically. 'That's funny!'

'What are you laughing about?'

'There's not a hope in hell you can thwart me now, John dearest — not without killing your darling child! Of course you must have the lantern.'

Sarah shivered. Her teeth chattered like castanets. Cold damp air, a smell of rot, wafted from the darkness of the tunnel.

Her father raised the lantern and its light showed walls grey with slime. Silvery mould grew on sagging logs that supported the roof. She felt in more danger than ever. But her father paid no regard to the perils of the surroundings.

They went in.

Lorraine seemed hasty and somehow triumphant, quite unaffected by the death of her hired detective, Hopkirk. Compunction didn't exist for her. The man had been despicable, but Sarah shuddered anew when she thought of his dead body lying on the plank floor above them, oozing blood.

At places, the passageway was less than head height and they were forced to stoop. It trended deeper in fits and starts and the phrase 'bowels of the earth' came to Sarah and stuck, drumming in her aching head.

The lantern's light showed the rock walls were veined with thin strata of pure gold which she suspected would have been judged a hugely profitable strike in any other mine. Wondering why not here, and why the gold had been left behind, she recalled hearing old reports of the problems the operators had struck with cave-ins and flooding.

Given the condition of the timber shoring and the pools of water they were treading through, it wasn't a reassuring thought.

Eventually, they came to a widening in the shaft, a kind of cave where the walls were further apart, the roof higher and signs of past activity more plentiful. Maybe this was where work had ceased at the time of the mine's abandonment. A stack of tools leaned against the rough walls — picks, shovels, sledge-hammers of varying weights, crowbars.

The bases of the walls were littered with rock chips. Water seeped in everywhere and Sarah found she was standing in a squelchy morass. There was also a sound of dripping water.

She ventured to speak.

'Isn't this dangerous, Dad?'

Snyder looked up as though he had to consider the notion. The water was mostly coming through cracks in the rock of the ceiling.

He said in a jollying way, 'Oh, it always leaks some when there's a heavy rain.'

'Enough chit-chat!' Lorraine snapped. 'Where's the money hidden?'

'Why, it's buried right here, Lorraine. You should curb your impatience.'

He pointed to a patch at shoulder height in the wall. It seemed to bulge and showed signs of disturbance that made it several shades darker than the surrounding rock. Though irregular it was about five hands square, about the size to take comfortably a knapsack packed with Treasury bills. And it was marked by heavy iron spikes that had been driven into the surrounding rock. The spike tops had once been painted red, though rust now predominated.

'Do you dig it out or do I?'

'Don't fun with me, John. Get on with it!'

Snyder hung the lantern on one of the spikes, turning up its wick and adjusting it so light was thrown on to the interesting bulge. He took up a pickaxe and hefted it.

Lorraine sucked in a sharp, excited breath.

'Mind what you do with that thing! Any accidents and Sarah is dead.'

Snyder swung the pick. The rock was soft and a hefty chunk rolled down and struck against his foot so he had to kick it away. He swung harder the second time, throwing all his weight behind the blow and hitting the same place again.

Thunk!

But the uncovered target was very wet this time. Only a small piece of detritus was dislodged, making a sucking, gurgling sound.

Before the ominous significance of this could register with his surprised watchers, Snyder swung again.

The third strike did it. The thud was followed by a rushing of water . . . and a chunk of rock was propelled into the shaft by a brown torrent freighted with dirt and stones.

'*Go, Sarah, go!*' Snyder yelled.

But Sarah was already moving. Of the two women, she was the first to recover from the shock of the geyser-like eruption into the shaft they occupied.

Lorraine was screaming, 'What have you done?' when Sarah sprang away from her a split-second before she tightened her finger on the trigger of her gun. The bullet ricocheted off the fractured wall.

The echoes of the shot were ear-shattering in the rocky confines but they were swallowed up by the swelling roar of the frothing gush that hurtled across the passage from the hole Snyder had hacked in the wall.

The recoil of Lorraine's heavy revolver was just enough to make her lose her footing in the slippery mud. She toppled, hitting the wall before landing in a splash and a sprawl and losing her grip on the gun.

Her scream was charged with hate. '*You bastard, Snyder!*'

She scrambled to get up, slipped

again. She uttered a strangled, spluttering cry.

Sarah saw her livid face, contorted with fury at being cheated of a fortune, go under the rapidly rising flood. Then her father was thrusting the lantern into Sarah's hands. The water was coming to their knees.

'Out! The way we came!' he commanded. 'Or you'll drown, too.' Though he was the creator of their predicament, naked fear was in his voice.

The increasing roar of the water was like a huge rapids or fall, magnified by the tunnel's enclosure. Sarah tried to hear the rest of the words her father flung at her, but she couldn't. She could see his mouth move, see the words formed, but she couldn't hear them. It was as though she was deaf. She tried to lip-read, but could make out only that he was exhorting her to flee. Which was the obvious thing to do anyway.

Sarah obeyed, thinking her dad would follow. The water was above her thighs and she was wading through it at the passage's higher level, almost to the cellar, before she gave a thought to turning.

Her father wasn't behind her. He was nowhere in sight. Back at the limits of the lantern-light's reach, the top of the tunnel went below the level of the dark, swirling water.

★   ★   ★

Sam was watching anxiously when Sarah climbed from the cellar. He was trying to bandage his chest tightly with strips of torn shirt to stop the bleeding. He thought a right rib or two was possibly cracked.

'What the hell's happened down there? I was frantic with worry. I heard a roar of water, maybe a shot.'

Sobbingly, gaspingly, Sarah told as much as she knew.

'Glory be . . . ' Sam breathed. 'Thank God you've got out.'

'I think my father must have fallen,

like my aunt,' she added weakly.

But another accounting for John Snyder's loss in the flooded tunnel occurred to Sam.

With his criminal career exposed to everyone — including Sarah who would have had to face the harrowing, shameful consequences of trial, imprisonment and possible hanging — he'd seen death and disappearance in the watery mystery of Horsehead Mine as a more acceptable alternative.

It didn't take an expert to figure out that Snyder must have come to know the geography of the mine as well as its erstwhile developers. The tunnel had evidently run close, very close, to a parallel shaft or tunnel that was flooded. After the storm's deluge, the pressure at the weak point in the membrane of rock between the two places would have been enormous.

Capitalizing on his knowledge, Snyder had precipitated the inevitable, the water had broken through, flooding more of the mine and hiding forever his guilty secrets. Sam predicted it was only a matter of time before every shaft and tunnel in the ill-conceived workings would be flooded.

After a last, fruitless inspection of the black pit of icy water beyond the cellar, they left for Rainbow City.

From a distance came a dying rumble of the departing thunder. The storm was over. The rain had stopped and the scent of wet greenery filled the night air, pungent but clean.

Sam delivered Sarah into the care of the shocked housekeeper at the Diamond S.

'Her papa's had a terrible accident,' was all he told the plump and fussing servant woman.

Sarah's warm hand squeezed his. 'Thank you, Mr Hammond. Hard and soft, you are both things.'

★   ★   ★

Another time, several days later, when Sarah called on Sam at his office in

Rainbow City to thank him and seek advice on the forthcoming coroner's hearing, she also said, 'And Mr Hammond, perhaps you could tell Cl — *Mr Freeman* that I've never been too proud to spurn a sheriff's deputy, but he'll have to get his tongue untied first.'

Sam nodded understandingly. She was a good girl, nice-looking, basically honest and sincere. That her father had turned renegade and ended up with blood on his hands was no fault of hers — merely a cross she'd had to bear. If she'd inherited any characteristics from him, they were pride and pluck, no bad traits.

He was glad Sarah was looking forward, not backward. It was a healthy sign. He resolved to help her out.

'Cupid with whiskers . . . it's plumb loco,' he muttered to himself after she'd left the office.

Yet more time later — three months, in fact — Sam was best man at the wedding of Sarah and Clint Freeman.

It was good to see Sarah was over the

bad times and to know that she was inheriting both the Triple S and the Diamond S, reuniting her grandfather's ranching empire once parts had been sold off to pay the creditors.

Clint was no longer serving as a deputy. 'How's rassling cows these days?' Sam joshed him.

'Can't complain too much. Beats sheriffing all hollow.'

Sarah kissed Sam after the marriage ceremony, and said they would ask him to be the godfather of their first-born.

Sam got to thinking again about retirement. Maybe some time not too far off he could go fishing with a fine godson . . .

THE END

We do hope that you have enjoyed reading this large print book.

Did you know that all of our titles are available for purchase?

We publish a wide range of high quality large print books including:
Romances, Mysteries, Classics
General Fiction
Non Fiction and Westerns

Special interest titles available in large print are:
The Little Oxford Dictionary
Music Book, Song Book
Hymn Book, Service Book

Also available from us courtesy of Oxford University Press:
Young Readers' Dictionary
(large print edition)
Young Readers' Thesaurus
(large print edition)

For further information or a free brochure, please contact us at:
Ulverscroft Large Print Books Ltd.,
The Green, Bradgate Road, Anstey,
Leicester, LE7 7FU, England.
Tel: (00 44) **0116 236 4325**
Fax: (00 44) **0116 234 0205**

HELL'S COURTYARD

Cobra Sunman

Indian Territory, popularly called Hell's Courtyard, was where bad men fled to escape the law. Buck Rogan, a deputy marshal hunting the killer Jed Calder, found the trail leading into Hell's Courtyard and went after his quarry, finding every man's hand against him. Rogan was also searching for the hideout of Jake Yaris, an outlaw running most of the lawlessness directed at Kansas and Arkansas. Single-minded and capable, Rogan would fight the bad men to the last desperate shot.

SARATOGA

Jim Lawless

Pinkerton operative Temple Bywater arrives in Saratoga, Wyoming facing a mystery: who murdered Senator Andrew Stone? Was it his successor, Nathan Wedge? Or were lawyers Forrest and Millard Jackson, and Marshal Tom Gaines involved? Bywater, along with his sidekick Clarence Sugg, and Texas Jack Logan, faces gunmen whose allegiances are unknown. The showdown comes in Saratoga. Will he come out on top in a bloody gun fight against an adversary who is not only tough, but also completely unforeseen?

PEACE AT ANY PRICE

Chap O'Keefe

Jim Hunter and Matt Harrison's Double H ranch thrived . . . till their crew marched away to war's glory, and outlaws destroyed everything and murdered oldster Walt Burridge. When the war ended, the two Hs started over. However, for Jim, war had wrought changes beyond endurance. So Jim rode out and into the arms of his wartime love, the gun-running adventuress Lena-Marie Baptiste. Now, trapped by his vow to avenge Old Walt, he must choose between enmity and love, life and death.

SIX DAYS TO SUNDOWN

Owen G. Irons

When his horse is shot dead, Casey Storm is forced to brave a high plains blizzard. Stumbling upon a wagon train of Montana settlers, he helps them to fight their way toward the new settlement of Sundown. But gunmen hired by a land-hungry madman follow. Now the wagon train's progress seems thwarted by their pursuers and the approaching winter. With only six bloody days to reach Sundown, will Casey's determination win through to let them claim their land?

MISTAKEN IN CLAYMORE RIDGE

Bill Williams

Ben Oakes had always been involved in trouble — he'd killed men before — but now he was determined to live a new life and never to carry a weapon. But when he's wrongfully imprisoned for the murder of Todd Hakin, he's desperate to clear his name and escape the hangman's noose. Then Ben is finally released, and his search for Todd's killer leads him to Claymore Ridge, where he faces threats to his life from more than one quarter . . .